CAROLINE

CAROLINE

Jasmine Cresswell

G.K.HALL &CO.
Boston, Massachusetts
1990

Published in Large Print by arrangement with
Curtis Brown, Limited.

G. K. Hall Large Print Book Series.

Set in 16 pt. Plantin.

Library of Congress Cataloging-in-Publication Data

Cresswell, Jasmine.
    Caroline / Jasmine Cresswell.
        p.   cm.—(G.K. Hall large print book series) (Nightingale
series)
    ISBN 0-8161-5043-5 (large print)
    1. Large type books.   I. Title.
[PR6053.R467C37   1990]
823'.914—dc20   90-4771

Chapter One

THE Comtesse de la Rivière walked briskly across the soft carpet of her drawing-room. At this early hour of the evening the card-tables were still empty, and there was no need for her to waste precious time drifting from corner to corner with an air of melancholic languor.

Miss Caroline Adams, who was arranging the silver candelabra so that the maximum benefit would be derived from the costly wax candles, paused in her task. Even after eight years in the Comtesse's household Caroline still felt a surge of reluctant admiration every time she observed the consummate acting skills of her stepmother. There were few people, thought Caroline, who realised that the Comtesse concealed a will of iron behind a mask of fluttering femininity. How many women could run a gambling casino at a profit, and yet present London society with the convincing image of a fragile French aristocrat, incapable of distinguishing between a game of faro and a rubber of whist.

It was more than three years since the Comtesse had first opened her select gaming establishment at the most fashionable end of Mount Street, and the venture continued to progress from strength to strength. The alluring presence of Miss Adams, an acknowledged toast of the *beau monde* for three seasons, was considered by the knowledgeable to be one of the main reasons for the Comtesse's unqualified success.

Few people now bothered to remember that the exquisite Miss Adams was actually the Comtesse's stepdaughter, and there was certainly nobody to remind them. The Comtesse's marriage to an obscure Colonel Adams had naturally made no great stir in the waters of London society, and all thought of it had now passed from society's memory almost as completely as it had passed from the mind of the Comtesse herself.

In the four years since Colonel Adams's untimely death, the Comtesse had cultivated an exotic foreign image which would have sat ill upon the shoulders of a mere Mrs Adams, military widow. With the un-assailable logic of the single-minded, there-fore, the Comtesse had dismissed Colonel Adams from her thoughts. Only the parish records of St. Giles Church, Gillingford, still bore mute testimony to her brief exis-tence as the second Mrs William Adams.

As far as the Comtesse was concerned the marriage had been a romantic aberration, wholly out of keeping with her practical French nature. For two days after Colonel Adams died, she locked herself in her bed-chamber and refused all entreaties to emerge. On the third day she attended the funeral shrouded from head to foot in black mourning-veils, so thick that her features were virtually invisible. On the day after Colonel Adams was buried she shed her mourning clothes and resumed her for-mer title. She was now known, to herself and to the *ton*, as a delicate female struggling to recover from the emotional ravages suf-fered during Robespierre's Reign of Terror.

The existence of a twenty-five-year-old English stepdaughter did not fit well with this pitiable self-portrait. Fortunately for Caroline, since her father had left her with-out a feather to fly with, the Comtesse did not consign her stepdaughter to the general oblivion which shrouded her years with Colonel Adams. When the Comtesse embarked upon her new career, Caroline was graciously included in the project. With more than a touch of wry amusement, Caroline resigned herself to a new rôle as an unidentified 'connection' of the Comtesse, whose chief function was to glamorise her stepmother's ruinously expensive gaming-tables.

Sometimes the fantasies woven by the Comtesse became so compelling that Caroline found herself losing touch with the threads of her former life. The passage of every month made it more difficult to remember that there had once been a different Caroline Adams, brought up to a set of values quite alien to those of the Comtesse. Brought up, moreover, by a mother who would have swooned with lady-like horror at the thought of *her* daughter presiding over a faro-bank.

Caroline sighed at the trend of her thoughts, then glanced up and caught the Comtesse's uncomfortably penetrating gaze fixed upon her. She smiled slightly, twisting her shoulders in a humorous gesture of resignation, and put the last candelabra on the table with deliberate calm. It was evident that her stepmother was preparing to deliver a lecture.

Whatever the Comtesse had meant to say remained unuttered, for the door to the saloon burst open and a handsome young man swept into the room, dipping into a deep bow as he reached Caroline's side.

'My love, my dearest!' He smiled at her with an appealing, boyish charm, seizing her hands and raining kisses upon the tips of her fingers. 'Did you think I had forgotten? I am only late because I have searched the four corners of London to bring you the gift most suited to your incredible beauty.'

With a flourish, he produced a small velvet box from the hidden pocket in his evening-coat. 'Try it on, Caro! It will look perfect with that blue dress you're wearing.'

Caroline accepted the box with a flush of pleasure.

'Philippe, you are a hopelessly irresponsible flirt.' Her smile robbed the words of all their sting. 'You had best stop flattering me and make your apologies to your mama. She has been worrying this past hour and more as to where you might be. You know

5

that tonight we are expecting a particularly large crowd.'

He pouted sulkily, looking younger than ever, but turned willingly enough to his mother. 'Ah, *Maman!*' Gently he took her hands into his clasp. 'How could you have worried? You knew I would be here.'

'Did I?' asked the Comtesse dryly, but she could not keep the glow of pride from softening her dark eyes. 'You are looking especially handsome this evening, Philippe.'

He turned round to display his excellent figure to full advantage. 'At least the English know how to cut a coat,' he said. 'And is Caroline's birthday not the perfect excuse for taking trouble with my appearance?'

Caroline opened the jeweller's box and looked at the sapphire pin, gleaming in its circle of diamonds.

'Philippe!' she said, her eyes shining. 'It's beautiful, and I appreciate your thoughtfulness.' Impulsively, she raised herself on tiptoe to drop a soft kiss on her stepbrother's cheek. 'Would you fix it on to my dress? Isn't it fortunate that I chose to wear the blue silk? We had better not stand together tonight in our new finery or we shall make all the old tabbies jealous!'

He smiled gallantly. 'You are bound to do that anyway, my dear. With golden curls and eyes of brown velvet, what can you expect? I hear tonight that Lord Carrisford is coming to visit us—and merely to satisfy himself that you are as beautiful as everyone says.' He placed his hand on his heart and winced with exaggerated pain. 'Ah! It is fortunate that I am your stepbrother and four years younger than you, or my heart would lie shattered at your feet!'

The Comtesse intervened sharply. 'You have several pieces of correspondence waiting for attention, Philippe. Since you haven't graced us with your presence for the last two days, you had better attend to such business matters at once. Besides, I have something to discuss with Caroline.'

Philippe bowed towards his mother with apparent deference and kissed his fingertips extravagantly to Caroline, wrinkling his nose as he walked through the door.

'I am glad to make my escape, fair sister. My mother is wearing her most disagreeable look. I have a premonition that you are about to receive one of her so-uncomfortable scolds.'

Caroline laughed softly. When Philippe allowed his voice to deepen with a hint of

French intonation, he was at his most irresistible. 'Unlike you, dear brother, I have
no guilty conscience. You may leave the
room quite safe in the knowledge that I
don't tremble at your mother's feet. On the
contrary, she probably wishes to do no more
than consult me about the inferior quality
of our salmon patties. Now go! wretched
boy, and catch up on your correspondence
before our . . . guests . . . are upon us.'

'Our guests!' He could not mask the sneer
in his voice. 'I could think of other words
to describe them. All right, *Maman!* There
is no need to look at me with such disapproval. I am going immediately. My papers
are as good as dealt with, so swiftly shall I
read them.'

The Comtesse waited until the door was
shut behind her son before turning to face
Caroline. 'Philippe was almost correct, you
know,' she said abruptly. 'Tonight I intend
to offer you my birthday gift, which is less
pleasurable than Philippe's, but perhaps
more useful. It is as Philippe said, you are
to have a lecture. Forgive me, Caroline, but
I have to share with you the benefit of my
years of experience.'

Caroline stifled a sigh. 'I must confess to
preferring the sapphires, ma'am,' she said

lightly. 'You know that where my future plans are concerned we usually cannot manage to see eye-to-eye.' Her face was lighted by a sudden flash of merriment. 'If I remember our last conversation correctly, I think you were finally reduced to calling down curses upon the heads of my Puritan ancestors.'

'Ever since your father mentioned to me that his great-great-grandfather led Cromwell's regiment of Ironsides, I have understood that there is an unfortunate taint of the bourgeois in your blood, Caroline dear. It quite explains these depressing fits of strange morality which overtake you at entirely inconvenient moments. Virginity and marital fidelity are concerns for merchants and Protestant clergymen. What have you to do with such miserable people?'

'Very little with clergymen and nothing at all with merchants,' said Caroline. 'But I cannot think most people would agree with you that faithfulness in marriage is *miserable,* ma'am. Unusual, perhaps, but surely still to be wished for?'

The Comtesse regarded her stepdaughter with an evident mixture of bewilderment and exasperation. 'Ah, Caroline! Sometimes I despair of you. For three years you have worked here with me. You have had endless opportunities to form an eligible connection, but still you rattle on to me about marriage and fidelity. Last time we spoke you informed me that you wished for love—and affection! How can you talk in such a fashion after all you have observed in these rooms?'

'It is sometimes a little difficult to remember that there are husbands and wives who are fond of each other,' said Caroline lightly. 'But I can always reassure myself by recalling memories of the happiness you and my father shared.'

'Bah!' said the Comtesse. 'Always you throw in my face my so-great stupidity with your father. Four years of trailing round military camps, and what did I have to show for it when he died? I had to pawn the last of my jewels to start this *salon*. Is *that* what you look for from life? A marriage scrimping and saving, and a widowhood full of memories and penny-pinching?'

'At twenty-five, ma'am, I am too old to pretend that I wish to be poor. But I should certainly prefer to remain single, if I cannot manage to fall in love.'

'That is very wise,' said the Comtesse. 'We are entirely in agreement. So let me tell you the point of this little conversation. Sir Geoffrey Hume has offered to make you a substantial financial settlement and provide you with the deeds to a snug little house in Richmond in return for your—er—that is to say, in return for your companionship. He has mentioned the sum of three thousand pounds. Do not tell me, I beg you, that you will not consider his offer. It is your birthday today. You have already reminded me that you are five-and-twenty. What do you hope for that you constantly refuse these excellent opportunities? At your age, you must consider that you cannot hope to retain your looks for ever. Today you are a ravishing virgin. Tomorrow perhaps you may be no more than a dried-up spinster, then what will you do?'

'I could always take to governessing,' said Caroline wryly. 'No, ma'am, don't bother to reprove me, I was not serious. What mother in her right mind would hire *me* to instruct her daughters?' She sighed, and then tried to laugh. 'You know, this proposal falls on an appropriate day. I am five-and-twenty, and this offer makes the twenty-fifth proposition I have received in the last three years. I have been keeping count, and Sir Geoffrey is the tenth gentleman this year who has been so obliging as to offer me a snug little house in Richmond. Diverting, is it not?'

The Comtesse could hardly conceal her impatience. 'I do not find it diverting in the least. Merely annoying. But you have not answered my question. May I tell Sir Geoffrey that you will consider his offer? You can see that he is a man of great sensitivity, for he made his approach to me rather than directly to you. I have not the least doubt that you would find him a charming lover.'

'Charming!' exclaimed Caroline. 'He cannot be a day under fifty.'

The Comtesse's hands fluttered in agitation. 'Caroline, I am very fond of you. Apart from anything else, your appearance reminds me of your father who was the most handsome man I have ever set eyes upon. But I cannot tolerate these missish humours any longer. For your own sake, Caroline, I must start to be a little stern with you. What does it matter if Sir Geoffrey is an older man? His position with the government makes him a gentleman of the first consequence. Do you wish your first liaison to take place with a callow schoolboy who has not yet learned how to treat a woman?' She sighed with dramatic melancholy. 'I fear that I have erred in my treatment of you, Caroline. Since your father died, I have been foolishly indulgent and allowed you to pursue a course of behaviour which is not in your best interests. It is true that I have derived considerable benefit from your constant presence here in my *salon*, but I should not have allowed this fact to cloud my judgment. I am issuing an order, Caroline. Either you will accept Sir Geoffrey's offer, or you must find yourself some other protector. I am no longer prepared to retain you in my household.'

'Dear ma'am, you cannot be serious!' Caroline hovered uncertainly between tears and laughter. 'You are trying to tell me that I have failed in my obligations as a daughter because I do not wish to enter into an illicit relationship with a man more than old enough to be my father! Please tell me that you are only teasing me?'

'Humour has never been further from my thoughts,' said the Comtesse stiffly. 'My life style is extravagant, and although this *salon* is quite profitable I have little hope of leaving you a significant sum of money. Such capital as I have will necessarily go to Philippe, who is far less capable of providing for himself than you are. I am a realist, you see. Philippe is my son, and I love him, but I suffer no delusions as to his weakness of character. In this, as in so much else, I deceive myself less than you do. Circumstances have conspired to make you an ineligible bride, Caroline. Can you not learn to adjust your life, as I was forced to adjust mine?' For the first time the Comtesse allowed a note of bitterness to creep into her voice. 'I was not trained to become a proprietress of a gambling-house, you know. I, too, have been forced to cut my coat according to the cloth I have available.'

Caroline felt a surge of sympathy, and placed her arm affectionately on the Comtesse's stiff shoulders. 'Indeed, ma'am, I could never cease to admire the courage you have always shown in the face of adversity. It is just that I seem to have a less adaptable nature than your own. I cannot help reflecting that my parents would never have agreed to the course you are urging me to follow.'

'Your parents are dead,' said the Comtesse flatly. 'You are now my responsibility, not theirs. There is no point in pursuing this conversation any further. My mind is made up. I shall be resolute in the face of opposition.' Her deceptively fragile features recomposed themselves into a mask of obstinacy. 'Nobody shall say that I am unreasonable. I do not insist that you accept Sir Geoffrey's offer. You may have until tomorrow evening to decide upon Sir Geoffrey, or to select some other man who can be your protector. I, of course, shall wish to examine the financial arrangements. It will be as well if the gentleman, whoever he is, realises that he has somebody other than a green girl to deal with.'

With a sudden flash of panic, Caroline realised that her stepmother was entirely serious. 'I cannot accept such an ultimatum,' she said urgently. 'I am grateful to you for all that you have done for me, but I cannot allow myself to be forced into a liaison that I know would be wrong.'

'That is as you wish.' The Comtesse allowed her natural acting ability to sweep her along. Now she was lost in the rôle of the tragic aristocrat. Her tiny, elegant nose lifted several inches higher in the air. 'Your future is yours to arrange as you wish. However, after tomorrow night there is no longer any room for you in my house. I shall send Clothilde to help with your packing once this evening's entertainment is finished. It is imperative that you realise the seriousness of your situation. I should be failing in my duty if I did not make this last push to see you satisfactorily established.'

'Good heavens, ma'am, no disaster threatens us, nor are you at your final prayers!' exclaimed Caroline. In her wrought-up state she failed to observe the sudden flush that suffused the Comtesse's delicately-painted cheeks. 'I will not allow myself to believe that you intend to bar me from your home!'

'This conversation is at an end,' said the Comtesse haughtily. 'Our guests will be arriving at any moment. I rely upon your good judgment. And the fact that you will certainly starve if you do not use it.'

She swept out of the room without a backward glance, leaving Caroline with nothing much to do except rearrange the candelabra and wonder if her stepmother could possibly intend to put her outrageous threats into action.

Chapter Two

CAROLINE was accustomed to thinking of herself as a cheerful soul, blessed with considerable common sense and an enviably practical nature. Having lived with the same face for twenty-five years, she was no longer startled by the astonishing beauty of her own features, and accepted the endless compliments on her appearance with a polite indifference that verged upon open boredom. If she sometimes sighed a little over the unexpected direction her life had taken, she was more often able to laugh at the endless stream of illicit propositions that came her way.

Tonight, as she greeted guests and laughed and flirted without an apparent care in the world, she realised that she was finally faced with the consequences of the decisions she had taken so lightly at the time of her father's death. She felt torn between amusement at her stepmother's unique moral code and a faint fear that this time the Comtesse was serious in her threats. She supervised the evening's entertainment, therefore, with less than her usual enthusiasm. Her concentration, never very fully centred upon the card-tables, was tonight entirely devoted to avoiding any chance of an involuntary encounter with Sir Geoffrey Hume. If Sir Geoffrey did not actually make his offer tonight, Caroline could plead with the Comtesse for more time. Given a few days to look around, she might find work as a lady's companion even if all positions as a governess were closed to her.

In fact, the evening's entertainment was in full swing before Sir Geoffrey entered the Comtesse's main saloon, and when he arrived he was not alone. He was accompanied by a tall man, quite unknown to Caroline, whose appearance was in marked contrast to Sir Geoffrey's old-fashioned addiction to jewels, fobs and laces. His dark coat was almost ostentatious in its severe plainness of line, and his air of unconscious assurance suggested a man who was accustomed to doing very much as he pleased and meeting little resistance to his ambitions. He was also, despite a singularly cold pair of grey eyes, quite the most handsome man that Caroline had ever seen.

She could not hope to ignore Sir Geoffrey's determined progress in her direction, so she bent her mind to the task of keeping him close by the side of his unknown companion. The presence of a stranger would surely prevent so conventional a man as Sir Geoffrey from making Caroline an illicit proposal.

She turned a radiant and insincere smile upon the two gentlemen, shaking her golden curls at Sir Geoffrey in a gesture of mock reproach.

'La, sir! The Comtesse and I thought our most faithful visitor had deserted us. Can it be that our card-tables are losing their appeal?'

Sir Geoffrey creaked into a deep and flourishing bow. Caroline held her breath, and hoped that his stays would survive the evident pressures being thrust upon them. Sir Geoffrey raised her hand to his lips with punctilious deference. His glance strayed once over the soft white slope of her shoulders and then turned politely back to her face.

'The card-tables have never exerted much attraction for me, Miss Adams,' he smiled gallantly. 'Your own fair person has always been the lure which brought me to the Comtesse's establishment.'

Caroline resisted the urge to snatch her hand away and rub it on the skirt of her dress. Instead she smiled coyly, and gently retrieved her fingers.

'La, sir, the Comtesse would be less than flattered to hear your praises. She prides herself on the excellence of our entertainment.'

She bestowed a dazzling smile on Sir

Geoffrey's silent companion, anxious to turn the conversation before her elderly suitor could be inspired to suggest a private meeting.

'You have not introduced me to your friend, Sir Geoffrey.' She fluttered her lashes behind the unfurled lace of her fan. 'You know how much I enjoy meeting new gentlemen, especially a friend of yours.'

Sir Geoffrey, in fact, had known nothing of the sort. Caroline's reputation as unapproachable—it was even whispered she was still a virgin—had been one of the main reasons for his offer of such a generous financial settlement. Run-of-the-mill mistresses could be had for a couple of hundred pounds cash and the promise of rented accommodation, but Caroline's aloof manner indicated that she valued her favours highly. However, Sir Geoffrey's understanding of women was not powerful. A widower of many years' standing, he confined his attentions to the women hovering on the fringes of society. He paid them well while he was with them, and dismissed them from his mind whenever business or other pleasures called. Consequently, he was quite happy to accept surface appearances, and to conclude that Caroline's startling change of manner was entirely due to her pleasure at the generous terms of his offer. Since it did not occur to him that a woman in Caroline's position might not be for sale, he congratulated himself silently on having pitched his offer just right. He knew she had turned down slightly less from Mr Beaumarchais, and he could not quite decide whether his extra thousand pounds, or the thought of his title, had finally tipped the scales in his favour. He smiled good-naturedly at Caroline.

'Lord Carrisford has come here just to meet you, my dear. He insisted upon seeing for himself whether your beauty lived up to all the tales about it.'

Caroline felt Lord Carrisford's gaze fix itself upon her, and she was aware of a sudden spurt of rage at the cynically cold assessment she saw unconcealed in his eyes.

'There are few beauties who live up to their reputations,' she said a little breathlessly. 'You gentlemen are such gossips, and delight in exaggerating our charms.' She felt irked by the conversation, resentful that the desire to avoid hearing Sir Geoffrey's offer should be forcing her into such inanities. 'Besides, I should prefer to be known for some other quality than the composition of my features. There is more to most women than a pretty face, you know.'

'Indeed, one always hopes so.' Lord Carrisford deliberately misinterpreted her trite remark. His insolent eyes roamed over her body, causing a flush to flood through her cheeks. His slight bow was full of mockery. 'I am Carrisford, and *entirely* at your service. You can be none other than the . . . famous Miss Caroline Adams.'

She ignored his suggestive tone as much as she was able.

'I seem to be better known to you than you are to me, my lord. I have not heard of you during the three years I have spent in London.'

'Perhaps we do not move in the same circles, Miss Adams.'

Sir Geoffrey, as if unaware of Lord Carrisford's insults, patted Caroline's arm patronisingly. 'No reason for a pretty little lady such as yourself to know about government matters. Lord Carrisford has been with Viscount Wellington in the Peninsula for over two years.' He smiled conspiratorially at his companion. 'We cannot expect such a pretty head to be filled with information about your diplomatic adventures, Carrisford. It is quite enough if she will but turn those enchanting brown eyes in our direction occasionally.'

'Certainly,' said Lord Carrisford dryly. 'Surely I did not create the impression that I expected Miss Adams to know anything about the battles raging beyond the borders of her cosy little world?'

Only the fear of being left alone with Sir Geoffrey prevented Caroline from uttering the scathing retort that hovered on her lips. As it was, she smiled at Lord Carrisford with false brilliance, her voice husky with the effort of controlling her anger. She forced out a trill of hard laughter.

'Oh, tut, tut, my lord! I know all about Spain and Portugal. I often think how fortunate it is for those ignorant peasants over there that our English gentlemen so much enjoy drinking port and madeira. Otherwise we poor females would be hard put to understand why anybody would want to fight in such a miserable part of the world. Why, only last week Colonel Matthews was telling me that the peasants there are so poor that they live most of the year on dried seaweed and garlic. I can scarcely understand why *British* soldiers need to fight to defend such people. Napoleon is surely welcome to such a wretched piece of country. Provided we could come to some arrangement about the port and madeira, of course.'

Lord Carrisford's mouth curved into a cynical sneer, and Caroline felt a spurt of illogical satisfaction. If he was determined to think ill of her, she would make sure that she blackened the picture.

Sir Geoffrey smiled, and an indulgent gleam appeared in his eyes. He expected all women to be unintelligent, or cold hearted, or quite possibly both. He was not at all put out by the discovery that his newly-chosen mistress had just shown herself to be callous and narrow-minded. His offer for Caroline had been made on the basis of her ravishing face and tantalising figure, and he had no interest whatsoever in the general tone of her mind. He laughed with unabated good humour.

'Well, Carrisford, that should cut you down to size! All your months of diplomatic negotiations reduced to a battle to preserve our supply of port.'

For a brief moment, Lord Carrisford's face was lightened by a wry smile. 'There may be more truth in that assessment than I like to think.' The trace of humour vanished as he turned to stare coldly at Caroline.

'Since my return to London, Miss Adams, I have heard a great deal about your extraordinary beauty. I can see that as far as outward appearances are concerned, rumour for once does not lie.'

Caroline paled slightly, but she refused to react to the insult. 'Thank you, my lord.' She smiled exactly as if he had bestowed a generous compliment upon her. 'I see that Philippe de la Rivière requires my presence. At least, I imagine that is what he intends to convey by those strange arm movements he is making in my direction. If you will excuse me, sirs, I must see what he requires.'

She curtsied with extreme formality to Lord Carrisford, and smiled sweetly at Sir Geoffrey. Now that she had seen her elderly suitor in the company of Lord Carrisford, his courtly kindness suddenly took on a fresh appeal.

The two men watched her swift progress across the room.

'A splendid-looking gal, don't you agree, Carrisford?' Sir Geoffrey could not quite prevent the note of possessive pride from creeping into his voice.

'I trust, sir, that you are not planning to add her to your list of acquisitions? My father always told me that he knew nobody who was a better judge of horseflesh or a worse judge of women than you.'

Sir Geoffrey looked flattered rather than offended. 'Well, well. I must say I have always prided myself on the state of my stables. As to the women . . .' He shrugged eloquently. 'If they look good across the supper-table and smile prettily before they hop into bed, what more can you expect?'

'Nothing, perhaps. One always hopes— against all previous experience—that one might find a woman whose mind and character are as appealing as her body.'

'Dreaming, my boy. Take the advice of an older and wiser man. And one who's been married, to boot. Never look for an intelligent woman. They're a disaster in bed and then they expect you to spend all your waking hours listening to them. I wouldn't say this to anybody else, but my wife was a regular blue-stocking, and she never gave me a moment's peace. If she wasn't rattling on about the latest Italian poet, she was dragging me off to see some exhibition of marble columns. What's more, she left me with three daughters to marry off, and not one of them with a face worth looking at. I used to say to Maria, if I wanted to have a

26

conversation about the state of the nation I could call on any one of a dozen friends. That's not what a woman is for.'

Lord Carrisford laughed. 'I am only too willing to bow to your superior knowledge. I, thank heaven, have not yet had to endure the married state.'

'Well, you'll come to it eventually,' said Sir Geoffrey gloomily. 'Don't know how you've avoided it so far. Between your mother and your sisters, I should have thought you'd have given up fighting it by now.'

'I have two brothers, sir, so that the provision of an heir is hardly necessary. And then my career is not conducive to settling down and selecting a bride.'

'But you're the eldest,' said Sir Geoffrey, unconvinced. 'Just you wait, my boy. Now that you're home and have a few months' leave, you'll find everybody is out to marry you off.' He shook his head morosely. 'May as well resign yourself, old chap, your head's for the noose this time. I'll try to stand up for you, but a mere godfather is nothing if your mother once gets on the trail.' He shuddered, evidently at some unpleasant memory of a previous encounter with the Dowager Lady Carrisford.

Lord Carrisford looked unperturbed. 'I have great confidence in my powers of resistance,' he said. 'Thirty-five years of living with my mother has honed my capacity for self-preservation.' His wandering gaze suddenly fixed itself upon Caroline. Even at a distance it was impossible to mistake the soft intimacy of the smiles she was exchanging with the dashing young man at her side. Lord Carrisford drew in his breath in a sharp exclamation. 'Did she not say that young sprig's name was de la Rivière?' he asked.

'He is the Comtesse de la Rivière's son,' said Sir Geoffrey. 'Why? Do you have some particular reason for wishing to meet him?'

'No. It is merely that . . . No matter. I am doubtless finding hidden meaning in entirely insignificant facts. Too much reading between the diplomatic lines.' He turned abruptly to Sir Geoffrey. 'May I offer some most undiplomatic advice that I trust you will not resent unduly? Something about Miss Adams and her place in this ménage renders me uneasy. Do not, I beg you, enter into any undertakings where she is concerned.'

'Your advice comes a few hours too late, Carrisford, even if I wished to heed it. I saw the Comtesse yesterday, and although she sighed and fluttered a bit about the innocence of her precious protégée, I've no doubt Caroline will be smiling her acceptance to me before the night is out. Her manner tonight suggested as much. Apart from the smiles she is always giving de la Rivière, Miss Adams is noted for being stingy in bestowing her favours.'

'Stingy in bestowing her favors?' Lord Carrisford's lips curled into a supercilious smile. 'Unless, of course, the price has been agreed beforehand.'

'Very true,' said Sir Geoffrey calmly. 'But we are already in agreement about the worth of a woman's smiles, are we not? And since I am quite prepared to pay handsomely in order to stand in Miss Adams's good graces, I cannot think why I shall not find her an entrancing diversion.'

'It is rumoured that she is de la Rivière's mistress, is that what you said?' Lord Carrisford continued to scrutinise Caroline and her companion, dragging his attention back to Sir Geoffrey with evident difficulty. 'My dear sir, you have not yet met Teresa, who came back with me from Lisbon. She is every bit as ravishing as Miss Adams, and she has one inestimable advantage from your point of view. She cannot speak a word of English. In any case, her life's ambition seems to be to lie upon a sofa and consume sugar-plums for which she has conceived an incurable passion since we landed in Plymouth last month. There is no danger in the world that she will irritate you with needless conversation. May I make a suggestion? I would like to have the privilege of offering you Teresa's services, and I would like to put in a bid myself for Miss Adams.'

'If I did not know you better, Carrisford, I would think that you were trying to cut me out. Caroline's all the crack at the moment, you know. Quite a feather in my cap to have secured her.'

'Indeed, I *am* trying to cut you out. But not for the ignoble reasons you are suspecting. Believe me, sir, I do not think you and Miss Adams would suit. Why don't we slip out of here before supper, so that I can take you round to Teresa's apartment? I am convinced you will be pleased that you have not put your offer for Miss Adams to the final touch, once you have seen what Portugal has to tempt you.'

'It is true that until now I have always preferred a woman with dark hair,' said Sir Geoffrey. 'Mind, I do not make you any promises, but if Teresa is all you say I shall withdraw from the lists where Caroline is concerned and you may make her whatever offer you please. Truth to tell, I have some heavy settlements to meet when m' daughter marries next month. I'll be well pleased not to have to come up with a cool three thousand. And Miss Adams would insist upon cash, I'm sure of that.'

'I cannot pretend that Teresa would constitute a major economy,' said Lord Carrisford apologetically. 'Along with her passion for comfits, she has a yearning for diamond baubles and similar trinkets. Still, even one or two thousand pounds can buy a pretty line in diamonds, and the lease on her apartment is already paid for this year. My dear sir, the more I think about it the more convinced I become that Teresa is the perfect choice for you. Let us escape from this nest of vultures, before Miss Adams can come to secure her prey.'

Sir Geoffrey cast a regretful look at Miss Adams, whose golden curls were now enticingly sandwiched between the dark heads of two admiring gentlemen. It was not entirely easy to regard Miss Adams as a vulture, despite the admonishment of his godson. Nevertheless, the thought of the silent—and economical—Teresa was definitely appealing. Lord Carrisford was already striding purposefully towards the door of the saloon. Sir Geoffrey sighed deeply and hurried, insofar as dignity would permit, to catch up with his companion.

Chapter Three

CAROLINE slipped out of the library where she had been talking to her stepbrother, and walked dejectedly up the stairs to her own bedchamber. She struggled to conquer a feeling of irritation. It was so typical of Philippe's flamboyant nature that he should buy her a lavish birthday present while leaving his debts unpaid. Of course, she had not really expected him to return all the money he had borrowed from her. Indeed, she hastened to remind herself, she had no wish for him to do so. But a hundred pounds, or even fifty, would have given her some small hope of independence. Respectable rooms could be rented in Harley Street for less than nine shillings a week, and would provide a suitable address from which to seek a position as a lady's companion.

Philippe, however, had nothing to give

her. Flushing with youthful embarrassment, he confessed that his own outstanding debts as always far exceeded his quarterly allowance. 'But there is no problem, Caroline *chérie*.' He had smiled at her engagingly, his dark eyes glowing as he looked earnestly at her. 'Tomorrow I shall visit the so-dreary money-lenders. My glorious expectations shall once again be laid before them, and you shall have your money.'

Horrified, Caroline refused the nonchalant offer. 'I may not always have been very well informed, Philippe, but I certainly know better now than to let you fall into the hands of the money-lenders. Besides, your mother would never forgive me, and rightly so. It is an outrageous thing to suggest.'

'No more outrageous than borrowing money from my sister and being unable to return it,' said Philippe with irrefutable logic. He dropped his eyes from her inspection and said casually, 'I have some pieces of my father's jewellery which I could pawn if you would like me to do so.'

Caroline shook her head firmly. She wished she could remind him of the sapphire pin, so recently bought, which would probably raise at least a hundred pounds if sold to an honest jeweller. But it was hopeless to expect Philippe to sell his birthday gift without giving him any explanation as to why she needed the money. She got up from the chair and crossed the room with a light step, hoping she would succeed in making her voice sound sufficiently casual. 'I have one or two pieces of my own,' she said. 'There is no need at all for you to pledge the family treasures your mother has saved for you. It was to prevent you pawning your father's rings that I gave you my savings in the first place.'

She squeezed his arm in a gesture of sisterly reassurance. She had been protecting Philippe for eight years, and it was too late to alter her habits now. She left the room hurriedly, before her brother could press for more information, calling out a strict instruction for him to forget all about the money he owed her.

In fact, although Caroline was not convinced that the Comtesse intended to carry out her absurd threats, she was determined to use her free time over the next few days to seek out respectable employment. She chided herself for not having taken such a sensible step many months previously. With a faint twinge of guilt, she acknowledged that she found the Comtesse's gambling establishment—for all its disadvantages—considerably more alluring than the prospect of life as a paid companion. She wished for the hundredth time that her mother's earlier training had been less rigorous. She could not help thinking that if she followed her personal preference she would find life as somebody's mistress considerably more enjoyable than life as a general dogsbody. It was remarkably inconvenient for a girl working in a gaming-house to have moral scruples that held her back from committing herself to a life of sinful luxury. A wry smile twisted her lips. Her Puritan ancestors had done their job well. She hoped their plump and self-satisfied ghosts were working just as hard at finding a solution to her problems as they were at strewing moral obstacles in her path.

She went slowly into her bedroom, her spirits sinking even lower at the sight of Clothilde stolidly folding linen in neat piles, and wrapping delicate silk evening-gowns between sheets of silver paper. Caroline wandered aimlessly around the room, unwilling to recognise the ominous significance of the maid's activities. She paid half-hearted attention to Clothilde's flow of

French chatter, not even caring when the maid, rendered clumsy by Caroline's absent-minded stare, spilled perfume all over the contents of one of the boxes. The smell of 'Fleurs du Printemps' wafted in overpowering waves around the bedchamber.

Clothilde immediately burst into floods of tears. Despite more than sixteen years' devoted service to the exiled Comtesse, she still believed that every misdemeanour would mark the end of her employment. As far as Clothilde was concerned, the ghost of Robespierre and the tumbrils of revolutionary Paris loomed at the end of every domestic mishap.

Caroline attempted to reassure the maid, and finally succeeded in conveying the message that spilled perfume was an inconvenience rather than a tragedy of the first order. Leaving Clothilde sniffing dolefully, she escaped into the hall corridor and breathed a sigh of relief. The events of the evening were beginning to exact their toll.

The sounds of an arrival at the front door interrupted the flow of her thoughts. She glanced at the tiny gold watch hanging from a chain around her neck. Two o'clock in the morning. It was late for visitors to arrive, even though the public rooms remained open most of the night. Fortunately, she was not responsible for entertaining such late-night guests.

She hesitated outside the door of her room, wondering if she was ready to face Clothilde and the reek of perfume. Even as her hand hovered over the door-handle a young footman hurried up the stairs.

'There is a gentleman, Miss, who wishes to speak to you right away. I have taken the liberty, Miss, of asking him to wait in the library, seeing as how he indicated to me that his business with you was of a private nature.'

Caroline turned pale. She could think of nobody save Sir Geoffrey who would call on her at this hour of the night. With a pange of dismay she resigned herself to the inevitable. She could not turn Sir Geoffrey away, so she would have to refuse his offer, an unpleasant task she had hoped to avoid. Caroline did not doubt that the Comtesse would be annoyed. But surely she would not literally turn her stepdaughter out into the street?

'Thank you, Jack,' she said calmly. 'You may tell the gentleman I shall be downstairs directly.'

She went into her room and ran a comb

hastily through the tumble of curls still clustered becomingly at the nape of her neck. She felt worn out and a little able to face the forthcoming interview. She twitched at the skirts of her overdress and stared with dissatisfaction at her pale cheeks. Accustomed to seeing utter perfection when she looked in the mirror, she decided wearily that she looked as bedraggled as she felt. That was probably all to the good. Let Sir Geoffrey see how washed-out she looked after midnight. It might, conceivably, dampen his enthusiasm for the proposition he was about to make.

The library was not used at night, and there was no fire burning in the grate. The air struck chill after the warmth of the heated downstairs hall. Cold enough to match his eyes, was the first disjointed thought which came into her mind.

'You!' she exclaimed, and then was appalled at the way she had spoken.

'You were expecting some other gentleman, no doubt,' said Lord Carrisford frigidly. 'I am sorry if I have disappointed you.'

'No, no! It was not . . . That is to say, I had no reason to suppose *you* would wish to seek a private interview with me. I cannot imagine what we might have to say to each other.'

'Can you not? I do not lay any claim to originality, Miss Adams. I have a proposal to lay before you.'

His contempt for her seemed so unconcealed that Caroline failed to suspect his meaning.

'Proposal, my lord?' Her voice was bewildered. 'I cannot imagine of what nature.'

'Come, come, Miss Adams. I cannot believe that I am the first man to aspire to your favours. Indeed, I know for a fact that I am not.'

'Oh, I see,' said Caroline. 'You meant that sort of proposal.'

'You must not sound so down-hearted, Miss Adams. It is not flattering to your prospective admirer if you appear so unwilling to hear the terms of his offer.'

'I am afraid there has been some misunderstanding,' said Caroline abruptly. 'I was expecting some . . . some other visitor. You will forgive me if I ask permission to retire. The hour is well advanced and I have duties to attend to early tomorrow . . .'

'Miss Adams, do spare me the display of your usual tactics for pushing up the price of the offer. Let us be plain with each other.

I understand you were prepared to accept from Sir Geoffrey a gift of three thousand pounds and the deeds to a small house in Richmond. I do not wish to give you a house, since I would prefer you to stay in town. You would have the use of a private apartment in my own townhouse. It is an unconventional arrangement, I acknowledge, but I shall be busy over the next month or so and would find it more convenient. I am not ungenerous. I would be prepared to offer you a cash settlement of six thousand pounds in return for a few months of your services. I expect to be returning abroad before the end of the year, and at that time we could renegotiate the terms of our agreement. Does this sound satisfactory to you?'

'No,' she said flatly. 'The terms are not acceptable, my lord. I am not, in fact, available for the services you have in mind. You will excuse me if I now retire. Perhaps I may escort you back to the card-rooms, where I believe you will find some refreshments still being served.'

He shrugged impatiently. 'I am not in the habit of haggling over terms, Miss Adams. I will offer you seven thousand pounds, but do not suppose that you may press your good fortune any further.'

'That is your final offer, I take it, my lord?' Her voice was dangerously quiet, a warning signal that her temper was about to explode if only he had known it.

'I have already said so.'

'Then I regret that I must decline your final offer. May I call one of the footmen to escort you wherever you wish to go?'

'I see that I have offended against the conventions you presumably feel should operate during discussions of this nature. Come, Miss Adams. Will you not admit that it is preferable to lay my offer openly before you, rather than to hedge it about with frilly phrases that cannot possibly have any meaning for either of us?'

'You mistake the matter, my lord. I do not object merely to the manner of your offer. Your proposals are entirely abhorrent to me.'

'You are an exceptionally beautiful woman, Miss Adams, and from my observations earlier this evening I would suppose that you can be a charming companion when you wish to be so. You did not know me until a few hours ago, so I cannot believe you have any personal objections to accepting my offer. Let me try, therefore, to express my sentiments in a way you will find more agreeable than this cold recitation of the facts. I happen to have with me a small diamond necklace, bought for an . . . acquaintance . . . who now has no need of it. May I offer it to you as a gesture of goodwill? A guarantee, if you care to think of it as such, that you will not find me ungenerous if you fulfil your side of the bargain?'

For a few moments the diamond necklace twinkled in his fingers. He evidently expected the sparkling stones to provide the final, irresistible lure. Caroline was afraid that she might either scream hysterically or faint from the pressure of rage which threatened to consume her. Although the three years she had spent in a gambling *salon* should have cushioned the blow to some degree, the fact remained that she was unprepared for such a blatant attempt to purchase her favours. None of the tactfully-worded proposals she had received in the past prepared her in any way for Lord Carrisford's arrogant and mercenary proposition.

She saw that Lord Carrisford had laid a jeweller's box of black velvet invitingly upon the small escritoire at her side, and she was forced to turn her back upon him. The impulse to strike out at his disdainful features was overwhelming, and she dug her fingers into the palms of her hands, willing herself back under control. The Comtesse, whatever her vagaries at the present moment, had been a loving stepmother. Lord Carrisford was a prominent member of the government and an evident leader in London society. She could not risk offending so eminent a nobleman who could, if he wished, spell ruin for the Comtesse and her establishment. Her anger would have to be channelled into more devious pathways to revenge.

Almost of their own volition, she felt her fingers reach out and close around the velvet box. She was not quite sure what she intended to do; she knew only that insults such as Carrisford had heaped upon her during this interview could not be forgiven. Her voice, shaking with suppressed anger, sounded unfamiliar in her own ears.

'This necklace is mine, my lord? It is very lovely.'

Her feet walked across the room and, with some astonishment, she saw her hands lift the necklace from out of its bed of padded pink satin. 'Perhaps *you* would close the clasp, my lord?' She simpered coyly. 'It is a pity there is no looking-glass in this room. I should like to see the effect.'

She raised her brown eyes, brilliant with concealed anger, to meet his cool, grey gaze. Her mouth curved into a provocative smile. 'You look so fierce, my lord. Surely I have not displeased you already?'

He shrugged easily, his features rearranging themselves into a patronising smile. 'How could that be? You have merely responded as I anticipated. I have a long experience with women and diamonds. They seem to prove an irresistible combination. Come, let me fasten the necklace. It will display to advantage against the perfection of your shoulders.'

Her coy expression faltered under the condescending indulgence of his glance, but she walked as steadily as she could to his side and held up the necklace. She felt the firm touch of his fingers against the back of her neck, and repressed the immediate flicker of sensation that ran through her. His hands lingered on her shoulders and he lifted a cluster of curls admiringly.

'Your hair is a delightful colour, and unusual to find with such brown eyes. I look forward to seeing you dressed in a manner that complements such beauty.'

'In a négligée, perhaps, my lord?' she asked bitingly, quite forgetting her new rôle.

He bowed courteously. 'The suggestion is . . . enticing.' He picked up the hat and cane which lay on a chair beside the fireplace and said briskly, 'I take it that we are now agreed upon terms and that I may expect your presence in my house shortly. May I send my carriage to collect you first thing in the morning?'

'You move too fast, my lord,' she said somewhat breathlessly. 'The Comtesse must be consulted and the . . . the terms guaranteed. I cannot be ready to move until the end of the week.' She would have to find herself other employment in the few days of freedom still remaining. There was some satisfaction in the thought that when he arrived to claim her she would already be safely on her way to a new job.

Lord Carrisford thought briefly, then lifted his shoulders indifferently. 'I shall, in any case, be busy for the next few days. It is perhaps as well if we start our new living arrangements when I have more time to devote to your . . . entertainment.'

She clenched her teeth together in order to bite back the retorts clamped behind her lips. It was impossible to speak. He seemed quite unperturbed by her silence. 'By the way,' he asked casually, 'are you well acquainted with M. de la Rivière? It seemed from your manner this evening that you are old friends.'

'We have known each other for several years,' she said curtly. She had no wish to expound upon her family relationships to Lord Carrisford. 'His father is dead, so he is now the Comte de la Rivière although he does not always use his title.'

Lord Carrisford paused in his progress towards the front door, leaning negligently against the arched entrance to the library. Caroline guessed that her casual answer was, for some reason, of considerable interest to him. But he made no more direct references to Philippe.

'There is one further matter. I would never attempt to influence your choice of friends, my dear, but I do want to make sure that we are clear upon one subject.' His tone of voice was bland, but his eyes shone with hard brilliance. 'When I make an arrangement of this nature, I expect to enjoy the sole use of my companion's services. What has happened in the past is, of course, no concern of mine. For the future, at least while you remain under my protection, I expect to be the *only* object of your devotions. I trust I make myself clear?'

'Admirably, my lord.' She clasped her hands behind her back, to hide their tremble. 'The hour is well advanced, my lord, and I do have duties which must be attended to in the morning. Will you forgive me if I retire at once?'

'But of course. I am, in any case, on the point of leaving. I shall call and see the Comtesse some time tomorrow. No doubt, after our interview, she will be sufficiently pleased with you to grant you some leeway in the performance of your duties. I shall naturally inform her that for the next two days you will not be permitted to entertain visitors in her public rooms.'

'And this is your definition of a generous protector, my lord?'

'I shall be generous with *my* favours, Miss Adams. I do not expect you to be generous with yours. I bid you goodnight, and the most pleasant of dreams. This has been a successful evening for you, has it not?'

The door closed quietly behind him, and Caroline derived the most intense satisfaction from picking up a large and expensive vase of Dresden china and hurling it with considerable force against the closed panels of the library door.

Chapter Four

'I CONGRATULATE you, Caroline, upon your excellent selection,' said the Comtesse contentedly. She settled herself more comfortably against the upholstered cushions of the chair, taking care not to crush the immaculate silk of her black dress. 'You were quite right not to settle for Sir Geoffrey Hume. Lord Carrisford will be in every way more appropriate as your protector. He is still in his thirties, old enough to be sensible, yet not too old to make you a delightful lover. Almost I find it in me to envy your good fortune!'

'You did not find Lord Carrisford's manner just a trifle overbearing?' asked Caroline, unable to eliminate the irony in her voice. 'You are not worried that I may find his treatment of me just a touch high-handed?'

'Lord Carrisford is of the nobility,' said the Comtesse loftily. 'Did you expect him to discuss the arrangements for your future over a cosy mug of porter? He expressed his offer concisely, but with complete understanding of my delicate sensibilities. I am sure you may expect every consideration in his treatment.' She put her exquisite piece of embroidery to one side, her satisfaction so great that it was evidently no longer possible for her to concentrate on the minute perfection of her stitches.

'With any luck, Caroline, your future is secure. You will probably remain with Carrisford for two or even three years, and I have no doubt he will pension you off handsomely. You are a prudent girl, and I imagine that you will be able to live in modest comfort for the rest of your days. Think, Caroline! Two years with Lord Carrisford and there will be no more need to fret and fume over pennies. You may even travel a little and see something of the world as you have so often wished to do. After all, the war with that peasant Bonaparte cannot last for ever.' She sighed with contentment. 'It is a *great* relief to me that you are going to be so *securely* provided for.'

Caroline turned to look at her stepmother with sudden suspicion. 'That is the second time within a few days that you have mentioned the need to provide for my future. What is this, Belle-mére? Why this unprecedented urgency to see me settled?'

'I have no idea what you are talking about, Caroline,' said the Comtesse uncomfortably. 'You are five-and-twenty and I . . . Well, I am several years older than that. Who knows what may transpire in France to alter our circumstances? There are events on foot . . . In short, I have simply decided that the time has come to provide you with your own establishment.'

'I do not believe you, Belle-mére, but I know you will not confide in me when your chin takes on that particularly obstinate thrust towards the ceiling. Please promise me that you will not hesitate to speak out if you need my help?'

'You are a sweet child, Caroline,' said the Comtesse with unaccustomed gentleness. She rose gracefully from the cushioned chair and went to stand by the fireplace, staring down into the glowing coals with unseeing eyes. 'I wish . . . I wish that I had been able to make other arrangements for you. Something more suitable for a young girl reared for many years as conventionally as you were. But enough! It is done. We are committed to Lord Carrisford.'

She turned briskly away from the fireplace and walked towards the door. 'It will be for the best, Caroline, you will see. After all, even if we could have found you a country parson or a merchant with a fortune tied up in sacks of flour, who is to say that you would have found such a married life any happier than life with Carrisford? Consign your scruples to the devil, my dear. It is perhaps easier to do so if one has survived a revolution, but once you have lived with Carrisford for a while you will wonder why you resisted my advice for so long.'

'That could be, ma'am,' said Caroline, deciding that this was not the occasion to inform the Comtesse that she had no intention of joining Lord Carrisford's household. She was conscious of a twinge of panic which gripped her somewhere in the region of her stomach. Her destiny seemed to be marching forward and she was able to do so little to stop it. She stooped down and picked up a skein of embroidery silk that had fallen behind the chair. Her face was hidden from the Comtesse's view.

'I have been collecting together some of my old family mementoes, ma'am, and I have been wondering about my father's old duelling pistols. Do you remember where

51

we put them when we moved into this house?' She retrieved the skein of silk and placed it tidily in the Comtesse's work basket. 'I thought, with your permission, that I might take them with me when I go to join Lord Carrisford.'

Her voice sounded somewhat breathless, perhaps from the exertion of reaching under the chair. 'Lord Carrisford has already given me a present of diamonds. I should like to have something to give him in exchange.'

'An excellent idea,' said the Comtesse approvingly. 'The pistols belonged to your grandfather and should, therefore, be given to you. I will ask Sam to fetch them down from the boxroom and he may check to see that they are in good working order. It would not do to offer Lord Carrisford something shoddy.'

'Indeed not,' said Caroline. 'Everything for his lordship must be of the very best.'

'That being so, it is flattering, is it not, that he has selected *you?*' said the Comtesse quietly.

'It is merely a compliment to the arrangement of my features,' said Caroline. 'My face is not me, you know.'

'Indeed not,' said the Comtesse. 'And

Lord Carrisford will think himself exceptionally fortunate when he discovers that your character is as attractive as your features.'

'What makes you suppose that Lord Carrisford will have any interest in getting to know me?' asked Caroline bitterly. 'I do not imagine that he plans to spend much time in idle conversation.'

The Comtesse turned a pale face towards her stepdaughter. 'Oh, Caroline! Do not hate me! I have only done what I must. There is no money for me to give you, and who will look after your interests if I should happen not to be here? Not Philippe, although it is his duty. He may smile and charm you and bring you gifts now, but his character is still untested, and who can tell how he will behave in a crisis? Do not be disappointed, Caroline, if your stepbrother fails to give you the support you deserve. My life has depended upon my clear thinking, and I have learned to judge character without sentimental blinkers to hamper my vision. When we were trapped in Paris by the Terror, my husband trusted his valet to bring us to safety. The man had served our family for thirty years and seemed devoted to our cause. I could not bring myself to trust him, however. I sensed some twist in his nature. So I lied about my plans for escape; I did not even confide the truth to my husband. I had my child to think of.' The Comtesse smiled sadly. 'My suspicions were correct, of course, but for a long time that knowledge did not bring me much consolation. I, cynic that I was, lived free in London, while my husband paid for his trust by giving his life for the entertainment of the Paris mob.' She dashed a hand across her eyes. 'Ah! I do not know why I speak such nonsense to you today. Go to Lord Carrisford, Caroline, as soon as you may. He has honest eyes.'

Caroline pressed her cheek shyly against the perfumed pink softness of the Comtesse's face. Her stepmother was not much in favor of demonstrations of emotion. 'Belle-mère, do not trouble yourself. I feel nothing but gratitude for your years of kindness to me. If we do not . . . If we have not always seen eye-to-eye on the question of my future, I promise you that I understand the good sense of your plans for me. I am only concerned as to the reasons for this sudden desire to see me settled.' She waited hopefully, in case her stepmother might decide to confide the true motives for her unexpected ultimatum, but the Comtesse remained silent. Caroline did not pursue her question, but gave the Comtesse another quick hug. 'Do not trouble yourself any more, Belle-mère. Whatever happens between Lord Carrisford and myself, I shall always hold you in deepest affection.' She escorted the Comtesse back to the fireside chair. 'I am going to ask Clothilde to bring us some tea, then I must go and complete the last of my packing. Lord Carrisford will be sending his carriage for me early on Saturday morning, I expect. Don't worry, dear ma'am. I shall look closely at Carrisford's honest eyes and forget all about his arrogant shoulders.'

The Comtesse smiled faintly. 'There are worse faults than arrogant shoulders, my dear. Go now and finish your packing, Caroline. There is no need to remain here, since I know that you do not enjoy drinking tea. Send Sam to me, if you please. The pistols shall be delivered to your room before you leave on Saturday. Do not bother to say a special farewell. I look forward to receiving a visit from you when you are comfortably settled.'

'I shall do as you say, ma'am. If Philippe has a moment to spare when he arrives this evening would you ask him to come up and see me? I shall have no opportunity of asking him myself, since I have been confined to quarters by Lord Carrisford.'

The Comtesse flinched slightly at the edge of resentment which Caroline could not keep out of her voice, but she spoke evenly enough. 'Philippe will be given your message, Caroline. I have one further favour to ask you, however. Do not tell Philippe of your intention to join Lord Carrisford. It is better if your departure is a *fait accompli* before he learns where you are. If he knows what we are planning, he will rant and storm about the family honour and about the sanctity of preserving your innocence, but he will have no practical solution to give either of us.' She looked at Caroline with unexpected helplessness in her eyes. 'Do not throw all of us into a turmoil for no purpose, my dear.'

Caroline was silent for a moment, wondering whether to give the desired promise and thus to abandon her last hope of help within the Rivière household. She looked carefully at her stepmother's face and saw for the first time the lines of strain and pallor that could no longer be concealed behind the Comtesse's exquisitely applied maquillage. She knew that her stepmother enjoyed excellent health, and she wondered yet again what mental strain could be causing these new lines of worry.

'Don't be concerned, Belle-meère,' she said quietly. 'Philippe shall learn nothing of my new occupation until you choose to tell him.'

Lord Carrisford's proposition had been delivered upon Tuesday. His proposals were formally accepted by the Comtesse on Wednesday, and Caroline's departure for Carrisford House was scheduled to take place early on Saturday morning. This left her with two days in which to find herself some gainful form of employment. Despite the advice of her stepmother, Caroline remained steadfast in her belief that she would prefer the life of paid companion to an elderly lady to the life of paid plaything for Lord Carrisford. Her bed might not be so comfortable in the old lady's house, but her conscience would permit her to sleep more restfully.

By Friday evening, however, bone-weary from an endless round of the domestic employment agencies, Caroline was almost prepared to acknowledge defeat and accept the fate urged upon her by the Comtesse.

Hard-eyed proprietors at the respectable establishments listened to her requests for employment with scarcely-masked incredulity. She felt her qualifications wither into insignificance beneath their scornful gaze. Not for the first time in her life, she cursed the evil fates which had decreed that her Mama's perfection of complexion should be combined with her Papa's classical beauty of features to produce a daughter of truly ravishing beauty. The angel who had wrapped this seductive exterior round a character that descended in an unbending line from great-great-great-grandfather Puritan undoubtedly suffered from a warped sense of humour. At the moment, Caroline was in no mood to appreciate the angelic joke.

The uncomfortable fact remained, however, that when Saturday morning dawned Caroline had nowhere to go except into the elegant comfort of Lord Carrisford's new barouche. Long before noon she found herself tucked up in the fur-lined warmth of its interior, watched by the Comtesse who was waving an affectionate but determined goodbye. Was it only her imagination, Caroline wondered, that detected heartfelt relief in the sudden slump of the Comtesse's shoulders as she turned back into the house?

Her over-active imagination had conjured up some vivid mental pictures of the style of rooms Lord Carrisford might provide for his concubine. Her scanty knowledge of the decor considered suitable for a love-nest, based largely upon discreetly veiled hints in Gothic novels, caused her to fear that she might be housed in a padded bower, lavishly draped in red satin.

No such baroque elegance was actually in store for her. When Caroline arrived at the Carrisford townhouse, an elderly maid of evident respectability conducted her up the private staircase to her new apartments. Caroline found herself in a set of freshly-painted rooms, comfortably equipped with modern furniture.

The maid was well trained and polite, even if there was no warmth in her manner. She offered to bring Caroline some refreshment and, when this offer was declined, set about unpacking Caroline's various trunks and boxes in a business-like silence which precluded any possibility of conversation. Perhaps it was just as well, thought Caroline. She had more than enough problems jostling for her attention without adding gossiping servants to the list.

She watched the maid until she could no longer tolerate the enforced inactivity. 'That is sufficient unpacking for the moment, thank you.' Caroline tugged nervously at the fingers of her French kid gloves, a parting present from the Comtesse. 'Your master . . . Lord Carrisford . . . is he at home at the moment?'

'I couldn't say, Miss, I'm sure. Lord Carrisford doesn't give me an account of his movements.'

The maidservant's response was polite, but some unguarded note of hostility caused Caroline to look at her sharply. She detected a brief flash of scorn in the old woman's eyes before the maid turned away to lay out Caroline's hair brushes on the dressing-table. Her task completed, the maid returned to stand in front of Caroline, her eyes downcast. 'Was there anything else, Miss?'

This time the maid didn't bother to conceal a note of disdain, but Caroline decided to ignore it. 'You haven't told me your name,' she said evenly.

'It's Bessie, Miss.'

'Well, Bessie, I am planning to go out. I have some shopping to attend to. Would you care to accompany me or would you prefer to send one of the other maids?' She looked challengingly at the servant. 'Naturally, I am not accustomed to walking in the streets alone.'

'Naturally not, Miss.' It was impossible to tell if there was irony in her words. 'I shall see what can be arranged.' Hesitantly, as if loathe to import any information to the interloper, she said, 'I think Lord Carrisford expected you to wait for him here, Miss.'

Caroline smiled with false composure. 'Really? But I am not in the habit of sitting around and doing nothing, Bessie. Perhaps you would see about sending one of the maids up to my room?'

'Yes, Miss. I'll see if Jenny can come up. She's not trained proper, but she can walk next to you and carry your parcels, I suppose.'

Caroline walked over to the cupboards and pretended to inspect her supply of bonnets with elaborate interest. 'Time is pressing, Bessie. I should be obliged if you would hurry.'

As soon as the maid left the room Caroline gave up her useless examination of hats and sank down on to the Louis XV armchair gracing the side of the fireplace. She soon realised that there was little point in staring at the empty fireplace. She needed to leave London and travel to a part of the country where nobody knew her. She sprang to her feet, filled with fresh energy. She would escape from Lord Carrisford and find herself a respectable job, even if it was necessary to dye her hair grey in order to secure it.

She hurried from the fireplace over to the dressing-table and took Lord Carrisford's necklace from its nest of pink satin. Just looking at the glittering strands of diamonds brought back all her feelings of resentment. How patronising . . . how *scornful* . . . he had sounded! She stuffed the shimmering jewels into her reticule, covering the diamonds with a wisp of lace handkerchief. Her mind was suddenly made up. She would sell the necklace and use the money to support herself until she found a job. She wished now that she had not wasted two whole days searching London for employment. She would have been more usefully occupied in arranging for the sale of the necklace and making her escape from Lord Carrisford's clutches.

A knock at the door interrupted her reflections. Her visitor didn't wait for her to call 'Come in!' before he walked into The room.

'I understand you are planning an afternoon out in town,' Lord Carrisford said. 'Pray allow me to escort you.'

'You!' She whirled round to face him.

He bowed ironically. 'You must strive for greater originality, my dear, since I am easily bored. You said the same thing the last time we met.'

'I wasn't expecting you,' said Caroline. 'I was expecting one of the maids.'

'I am confident that you will find me much better company. My purse is so much deeper than any of the maids.'

Caroline tugged nervously at the ribbons of her dress, unwilling to meet the cynicism of his eyes. 'I have no interest in the depth of your purse,' she said at last. 'I just hadn't expected my duties to start so early in the day.'

'No? But I don't think a shopping expedition is an onerous start to your new life.'

'My lord,' she said pleadingly, cringing inwardly at the sarcasm of his voice, 'I cannot think we shall suit. There must be many girls in London who would be willing, even grateful, to oblige you in every whim.'

'I don't wish to be indulged in every whim. In fact, Miss Adams, I find your antipathy positively intriguing. I am captivated by your irrational aversion to my presence. Why do you appear to dislike me so much when we know so little of each other? It is an interesting puzzle.'

'There is no puzzle, my lord. I am not accustomed to being treated as a . . . as a mere plaything for a man's amusement.'

'Then it will be entertaining to teach you your new rôle. I am sure we can come to some very comfortable arrangement—when you finally decide to be honest with me.'

Caroline's temper snapped. 'I have been honest with you! Let me warn you, my lord, I shall never submit to you. Never!'

Lord Carrisford looked at her through narrowed eyes. 'But you have already submitted, my dear, at least in principle. You did so when you accepted my diamond necklace. Now you have only to honour your bargain.'

'I have changed my mind,' said Caroline wildly. She tore open the strings of her reticule. 'Here,' she said. 'Take it!' She thrust the shimmering strand of jewels into his hands. 'I should never have come here. It was a dreadful mistake. I would like to leave now. Let me go, my lord! Please let me go!'

He laughed with genuine amusement, tossing the necklace on to a rug near the hearth. 'Lord, Caroline, but you're very good. Drury Lane has missed an accomplished performer in you.' He loosened his tight grip on her wrists and slid her arms down to her waist, clasping her in a casual and intimate embrace. 'I still can't believe this incredible hair,' he said softly. 'Are you sure that it's not as artificial as the rest of you?'

Caroline slipped out of his grasp and moved as far away from him as she could. 'I don't understand you, my lord. What have I said that is so amusing?'

Lord Carrisford smiled. 'Come along, Caroline. Pop one of those fetching bonnets on your curls and let us go shopping. I'm afraid the game is up this time before you really got it started. The Comtesse de la Rivière has already warned me about your acting ability. She told me that the rôle of an hysterical virgin was your speciality.'

Caroline turned pale, but her voice sounded quite steady when she spoke. 'I see that the Comtesse has been busy.'

Lord Carrisford's expression was cynical.

'The Comtesse was perfectly open about you, my dear. She did not want me to be put off by any of your protestations of virginal innocence.' He chucked her carelessly under the chin. 'If you are finally ready, I will summon the carriage.' He dropped a light kiss on her tightly-closed mouth. 'Such delicious lips! My sweet, you would have been quite wasted on Sir Geoffrey Hume. You should be pleased that you have come to live with somebody who is fully able to appreciate your charms.'

'Can we leave now?' She could not bear to remain cloistered in the room with him much longer.

'Certainly. You have only to choose your bonnet.' He tugged on the bell-rope and smiled at her with false friendship. 'You may entertain me in the carriage by telling me all about your friend Philippe de la Rivière. I am—intrigued—by the history of your acquaintance with that young man. Do hurry, my dear. I cannot abide to keep the horses standing.'

Chapter Five

CAROLINE believed her dislike of Lord Carrisford to be stronger than any emotion she had ever felt towards a man. She did not imagine, even for a moment, that she might be in danger of succumbing to the attractions of his personality. As far as she was concerned, he had no attractions. She was only prepared to be civil to him until she could sell the necklace and escape from London.

She quite failed to take into account Lord Carrisford's natural magnetism, his years of training as a diplomat, and his determination to lull Caroline into unguarded confidences. He cleverly kept the conversation during their carriage ride upon the most impersonal generalities. He chatted wittily about the newest plays and scoffed gently at the latest Italian soprano to burst upon the London scene.

Imperceptibly, Caroline relaxed her guard, allowing her natural interest and lively mind to give sparkle to her conversation. She forgot what Lord Carrisford was and why she was in his carriage, and gave

herself up to the luxury of stimulating conversation. Soon she was showering him with
questions.

'Were you actually there when Viscount
Wellington liberated the British settlement
at Oporto?' she asked. 'I have so much
wanted to hear a first-hand account! I read
that Wellington came upon Marshal Soult
while the Marshal was sitting and eating his
dinner! It is incredible that our soldiers were
able to avoid detection as they mounted
their attack.'

'It is amazing the lengths to which an
officer will go in order to get a good dinner,'
said Lord Carrisford dryly. 'Marshal Soult's
meal was not wasted, I assure you. The British officers sat down to eat Soult's dinner,
and very tasty it seemed after several days
of marching rations. Salt biscuits cannot be
recommended as a permanent diet, I fear.'

She smiled, but her expression tightened
as she remembered the aftermath of the
battle. 'I heard that conditions after the
fighting were very bad,' she said. 'The
newspaper accounts said that the sick and
dying were left by the roadside in pouring,
torrential rain. The French army executed
many of the Portuguese peasants as they

tried to retreat into Spain. Were the conditions truly as bad as we have heard?'

Lord Carrisford shrugged. 'The only wounded left by the roadside were ordinary French soldiers; common recruits from the gutters of Paris. And as for the Portuguese, they are only illiterate peasants, after all. I am happy to be able to reassure you that no harm befell any *British* officers. We lost less than seven hundred men in all.'

'Even French recruits and Portuguese peasants are human beings, Lord Carrisford. I have no doubt they feel hunger and pain just as we do.'

He looked at her in silence for a moment. 'This is a surprising change of heart, my dear. At our first meeting you told me that Portugal was too miserable a country to bother about. The peasants, if I remember correctly, were dismissed as eaters of seaweed. Now you are chiding me for expressing opinions no more callous than your own. I wonder why you are so deeply informed about the events surrounding the recapture of Oporto? And why are you so concerned for the welfare of the defeated French armies? Surely your interest in the safe supply of port does not require a study of Wellington's campaigns?'

She answered with some constraint. 'My father was a military man and I follow events in the Peninsula with interest. Then, too, the Comtesse de la Rivière worries about the course of the war. She abhors the successes of Napoleon Bonaparte and despises those of her compatriots who have gone back to France. I think she still cherishes the illusion that one day she will return to France and find that all is miraculously as it once was. She is always pleased to talk with me about the failure of one of Bonaparte's campaigns.'

'Her son, however, does not dislike the Emperor Napoleon.'

'Philippe?' Caroline turned to Lord Carrisford in amazement. His flat statement had suggested an almost personal knowledge of Philippe's opinions. 'I don't think Philippe is much interested in politics, my lord. He is at the age when the cut of his evening-coat or the pursuit of a pretty opera dancer occupies all of his attention.'

'Philippe de la Rivière is two-and-twenty, I believe. At that age, Napoleon had led a revolutionary army back into Corsica. I don't think age has very much to do with a man's political activities.'

'Well, my lord, for whatever reason it

may be, Philippe has shown no interest in politics.'

Suddenly conscious of having spoken too openly of family matters, Caroline turned and stared out of the carriage window. It was far too easy to fall into the trap of conversing freely with Lord Carrisford. She realised with a hint of panic that she ought to have set herself on guard against his attractions. This day had not proceeded at all as she had planned. Heaven forbid that she should complicate a difficult situation by starting to *enjoy* the hours she spent in Carrisford's company.

Lord Carrisford, after a glance at her heightened colour, made no attempt to press his questions. He smiled slightly. 'I'd better give the signal to the coachman so that he may stop the carriage. You haven't noticed, but this is the fifth time we have traversed the length of Bond Street.'

She was even more confused at this further evidence of how absorbed she had been in conversation. She was pleased to alight from the carriage, and glad to see the portly figure of Sir Geoffrey Hume waiting on the pavement close to the carriage steps. She smiled at him in greeting, ready to exchange a few polite words with him. She spoke his name, but he looked through her with deliberately blank eyes, turning to offer his arm to a dowdy young female waiting by his side. They walked briskly away, leaving Caroline standing with her hand still foolishly extended in greeting. The colour receded from Caroline's cheeks, but she said nothing.

Lord Carrisford tucked her hand through his arm in a gesture she found strangely comforting. When the groom had remounted the carriage, he said quietly. 'Sir Geoffrey was with his daughter.'

'I see,' she said. And indeed she did. Now that she had moved into Lord Carrisford's house, she had ceased to exist as far as the female members of society were concerned. Caroline stared rigidly ahead, hearing nothing of Lord Carrisford's conversation. Tonight, she resolved. Tonight, while Lord Carrisford dined out, she would leave his house. She had five golden guineas and the diamond necklace. Surely that would be sufficient to establish herself in some distant part of the country? Her brain worked feverishly. As a child, she and her father had visited some cousins who resided near Harrogate. She would seek them out and beg for their help in securing a respectable position.

Lord Carrisford's cool voice, faintly amused, broke in upon her chaotic thoughts. 'You do not seem enraptured by these shop windows, my dear. Would you care to look somewhere else?'

With an effort she focussed her attention on the present. They were standing outside a jeweller's. 'I don't wish for any trinkets, my lord.'

'No? Some new gowns, perhaps? Or a fur wrap?'

'No,' she said sharply. 'My wardrobe is perfectly adequate for my requirements, my lord.'

'No jewels, no clothes, no pleas for extra spending money. Exactly what game are you playing at, my sweet?'

She blushed hotly at the familiarity of his tones. 'I play for higher stakes than gowns and jewels, my lord,' she said angrily. Did he think all women could be bought either with money or with smiles?

Lord Carrisford's languid inspection of a sapphire ring ceased abruptly. He allowed his quizzing glass to slip out of his fingers and dangle once again at the end of its ribbon.

'The devil you do!' he exclaimed with a sudden bark of laughter. 'You continue to intrigue me, my dear. I suspected, of course, that you were aiming high. I didn't expect you to reveal your hand so early in the game.'

There was no need to feign bewilderment as she raised astonished brown eyes to stare into his cold grey ones. 'My lord?' she asked hesitantly. 'What do you mean?'

He tucked her arm familiarly beneath his own and started to stroll down the street. 'Don't spoil it by playing the innocent now. I find your frankness infinitely more captivating.' He wrapped her silk scarf around her shoulders with false solicitude. 'We must not allow you to catch a chill,' he said. Caroline could sense the mockery which ran like a shining thread through the depths of his conversation. 'Shall we walk to meet the coach? I asked the servants to tool the carriage up and down the street. Do you have any commissions for me to execute on your behalf, or may we drive to the Park?'

'I have no errands,' said Caroline in a low voice. 'Lord Carrisford . . . There has been a terrible misunderstanding between us, and I think we must put matters right before . . . before . . . I cannot return with you to

Carrisford House, my lord.' She seized her courage and looked him squarely in the eyes. 'I don't wish to be your mistress, my lord. I cannot . . . I have not . . . In short, it would not be possible for me to fulfil the terms of our agreement.' She found she could no longer meet the bland amusement of his gaze and dropped her eyes to the pavement. 'Would you purchase me a place on the stage to Harrogate, my lord? There is no reason why you should, of course, but if you would do this for me, and not reproach the Comtesse de la Rivière, I should be eternally grateful to you my lord.' Despite her best efforts, she could not prevent her voice cracking into a smothered sob. Her eyes glistened with the diamond drops of unshed tears.

'Why Harrogate?' asked Lord Carrisford interestedly.

She dashed a glove across her eyes and swallowed hard.

'I have cousins there, and I believe it is a place where many elderly ladies go to take the waters. I hope to find employment there, as a lady's companion.'

Lord Carrisford burst out laughing. 'Caroline, you are a treasure! I can scarcely refrain from kissing you right here in the middle of Bond Street. Until you mentioned the elderly ladies you almost had me bamboozled. I was even prepared to overlook your request for the stagefare when I paid seven thousand pounds into your bank account only yesterday. You are such a superb actress I was beginning to wonder if I had actually made some terrible mistake.' He looked at her with a smile. 'We could have a good time together, Caroline. I am beginning to hope my suspicions about you and young de la Rivière are without foundation. Why did you never go on the stage, Caroline?'

They were interrupted by a noisy shout of greeting before she could begin to think of a reply. Her heart sank as she saw Philippe striding towards them, his hands outstretched in greeting.

'Caro, my love! Where have you been all day?' Philippe, with a total disregard for the presence of Lord Carrisford, seized his stepsister in a fervent embrace.

Caroline dreaded the course that any conversation with Philippe might follow. She silently cursed the malevolent fate that had brought him to Bond Street at the same time as herself.

'We are not alone, Philippe,' she said at

last, hoping he would heed the note of warning in her voice. 'My lord, may I present to you the Comte de la Rivière? Philippe, this is Lord Carrisford.'

'I believe I have recently had the pleasure of meeting one of your relatives,' said Lord Carrisford as he executed a polite bow in Philippe's direction. 'By a strange coincidence, the man I met also styled himself the Comte de la Rivière. We met several times whilst I was in the Peninsula.'

Philippe turned white. '*You* have met him!' he muttered distractedly. With evident effort, he brought himself back under control. 'I regret to say that you are misinformed, my lord. The immediate members of my family were all killed during Robespierre's Reign of Terror in Paris. I and my mother alone escaped the fury of the mob. There are, I believe, some distant cousins who have survived the various changes in régime. Their branch of our family was politically and financially obscure, so they aroused the enmity of no-one. Perhaps Napoleon has seen fit to give these people the titles and lands that are mine by right. He has made other decisions equally as strange.'

Lord Carrisford inclined his head in what

might have been a gesture of apology. 'I regret if my remarks have caused you distress. It is merely that the likeness between you and the man I met is very great. I thought perhaps you were brothers. I wonder why Bonaparte bestowed your family lands upon such a distant heir? Perhaps he wished to reward your distant cousin for some special services to the government of France?'

'It is possible,' Philippe said curtly. 'I regret that since I am neither in the confidence of the Emperor Napoleon, nor my cousins, I cannot enlighten you further.'

He turned to his sister, deliberately excluding Carrisford from their conversation.

'May I offer you an escort to your destination, Caroline? You might prefer to come with me.'

She longed to accept Philippe's offer, but she was afraid of what Lord Carrisford might say. She put her hand in Philippe's and tried to smile naturally. 'We are expecting the carriage to arrive at any moment. I have no reason to trouble you further.'

'A service to you could never be an inconvenience, chérie.' Philippe bowed over her hand with unusual formality. '*Au revoir,*

Caroline. I hope I may look forward to seeing you at my mother's house this evening?'

She mumbled a non-committal reply, and as soon as Philippe passed out of sight she turned to Lord Carrisford, her face flaming with hurt and anger.

'How could you!' she exclaimed bitterly. 'How could you taunt him in such a fashion after all his family has endured! Oh, I only pray he has sufficient discretion not to run to his mother with this story! How she would suffer to think of her family home in the hands of relatives who have betrayed everything she holds dear! And her husband's titles wrenched away from Philippe by that upstart Bonaparte! Why did you choose to pass on such dreadful news?'

Lord Carrisford looked at her dispassionately. 'You must learn to control such displays of emotion, Caroline. You are attracting unwelcome attention with your heart-rending defence of your former lover. Perhaps you could strive to remember that *I* have now purchased your services and I do not expect you to question my behaviour. You may not like me very much, but console yourself with the knowledge that my finances are considerably healthier than Philippe de la Rivière's.'

'You are despicable,' said Caroline, throwing caution to the winds. 'Are you suggesting that Philippe was my lover? Nothing could be further from the truth. The Comtesse de la Rivière is my stepmother and Philippe is therefore my brother. We have been brought up together for the last eight years, and have known each other even longer. The Comtesse did not wish to broadcast news of her marriage to my father, and I have respected her wishes. I would not have told you, except that this is the second time you have accused me of an immoral relationship with my stepbrother, whom I have known since he was a scrubby schoolboy.'

For once Lord Carrisford was shocked out of his habitual hauteur. 'Philippe de la Rivière is your *stepbrother?* Good God, that cannot be so!'

She derived an irrational pleasure from watching his discomposure. 'What is so incomprehensible, my lord? Even harlots have mothers. Is it unthinkable that *I* should have a stepmother?'

'The information came as a great surprise to me,' said Lord Carrisford slowly. 'But I suppose there is no reason why our relationship need change.' He stopped speaking as the Carrisford barouche swept to a halt in the busy road. He stepped in front of Caroline to protect her from the dust thrown up by the carriage wheels. 'Did your stepmother never try to arrange a conventional marriage for you? Surely, with your looks, it would not have been hard.'

'The Comtesse is not great believer in the benefits of matrimony,' said Caroline dryly. 'She has reached a stage in her life when she finds well-lined pockets more appealing than moral purity.'

'And do you agree with her?' asked Lord Carrisford.

She looked up and saw the cynicism darkening the cool, grey depths of his eyes and knew that she would not tell him the truth. 'I am here with you, am I not?' she asked pertly. 'That seems to be the answer to your question.'

She derived intense satisfaction from the secret knowledge that before the night was out she would have vanished without trace. Her eyes sparkled with unshed tears, but she forced her lips into a jaunty smile.

'I believe the coachman wishes us to enter the carriage immediately. Come, my lord, you have told me we must not keep the horses waiting.'

Chapter Six

CAROLINE wrapped the folds of her dressing-gown more tightly around her waist and waited for the scurrying chambermaids to remove the last bucket of water from the rose-painted bath. Bessie, whose expression remained as dour as before, supervised the work of the young girls. When the maids left the room with the last of the water, the housekeeper walked over to the dressing-table and looked up at Caroline with carefully blank eyes.

'Do you wish for any further help, Miss?'

'No, thank you, Bessie.' Caroline felt hysterical laughter well up inside her, threatening to spill over. She bit her lip and turned hastily away from the maid's unblinking gaze.

'No,' she said more firmly. 'I shall not require any further service this evening. Please inform the servants that I do not wish to be disturbed—for any reason.'

'Very good, Miss. I trust you will sleep well, Miss.'

'Thank you, Bessie.' She ignored the unmistakable hostility in the maid's voice, and the housekeeper could do nothing except take her leave. Caroline sighed with relief when she heard the door close behind Bessie. At least she could now start her preparations for escape.

She glanced at the ormolu clock on the mantelpiece. It was already ten o'clock and soon the outer door would be locked and barred. Swiftly she went to the huge armoire and removed her cloak-bag, then reached under the bed to pull out the portmanteau she had already packed. She dressed hastily in a chemise and petticoats that still reeked of Clothilde's spilled perfume, and selected a warm walking-dress from the clothes Bessie had hung neatly in the dressing-room.

She tried to brush her wayward curls into some sort of respectable hair style, but her fingers trembled as she struggled with ribbons and steel pins. Her mind whirled in an endless circle. It seemed that during the evening she had already made and discarded a hundred different plans of escape. Now she had returned to the first and simplest one. She would go to her stepbrother's rooms and ask for one night's lodging. The Comtesse had wanted to keep the details of

Lord Carrisford's proposition hidden from her son. But Caroline knew she could not defer to her stepmother's wishes. She would have to tell Philippe most of her story because she needed his help in pawning the diamond necklace.

At last her hair was piled on top of her head, and she tied the ribbons of her bonnet firmly beneath her chin. Now that the moment of departure had actually come, she felt strangely calm as if all problems were over instead of scarcely begun.

She pulled out the dressing-case and the portmanteau. They seemed pathetically small containers to hold all her worldly goods. On an impulse, she walked into the dressing-room and picked up the elegant leather case which contained her father's pistols. She weighed the box in her hands, scarcely knowing why she had brought the weapons with her to Carrisford House. The weapons were heavy, but she was loathe to leave such a personal memento behind. There was no point in repining, however. There was going to be no room for sentimentality in her new life and no room for pistols in her portmanteau. She replaced the guns on the bed. Lord Carrisford was to have a parting gift, after all.

On tiptoe she crossed to the door, such caution was ridiculous, she knew, and yet instinctively she tried to shrink into the shadows, hiding herself from view. She turned the handle of the heavy door cautiously. One never knew how loudly such an old door might creak.

The door did not move. Less cautiously now, she rattled the handle, twisting and turning the iron knob with mounting urgency. It was several minutes before she would allow herself to accept the truth. The door was locked and on her side of it there was no key.

She sank down on the bed, conscious of the fact that her whole body trembled with outrage. A cold, hard fury started to consume her. She made to move towards the bell, ready to summon a servant and demand her release, but her hand halted even as her fingers reached out to curl around the velvet bell-rope. The schemes for revenge upon Lord Carrisford, until now only nebulous wisps of an idea, crowded into her mind. When she had asked the Comtesse for her father's duelling pistols, she had not seriously planned to use them. She had thought of them merely as protection, and ultimate weapon if events became too much for her. Even this afternoon, when she had been so angry with Lord Carrisford, she had only wanted to escape from his power. Now she wanted more.

With feverish haste, she scrabbled among the pillows and once again pulled out her father's duelling pistols. She would never be able to inflict upon Lord Carrisford the sort of mental humiliation which he had caused her to suffer over the past few days, but she could inflict a physical wound that would stay with him for months to come. With great care she set about the complicated business of loading and priming one of the guns, sighing with relief when the delicate task was finally completed. She tested the balance of the gun in her hand, reminding herself of the feel of this particular weapon. The aim of these guns was almost perfect, a fortunate fact since, even in her state of near-murderous anger, she did not want to have Lord Carrisford's death resting upon her conscience. She was a remarkably accurate shot, especially for a woman, but she would have to allow him to approach her closely before pulling the trigger. It was one thing to aim at wooden targets, rather different to take aim at a human being. A shiver of satisfaction ran through her. She imagined Lord Carrisford leaning over her, fondly expecting to receive a passionate kiss, and receiving instead a bullet in the shoulder. Caroline's eyes glittered with anticipated triumph.

There was truly a need for speed now. Hurriedly she pulled the walking-dress back over her head, tossing her bonnet high on to the cupboard shelf, and tearing ribbons and pins from the hair-style arranged so painstakingly only minutes before. She left on the chemise and petticoats, since she still hoped to make good her escape to Philippe's lodgings. She wondered if any of the servants would hear the shot, or if she could rely on the sound-deadening qualities of the heavy of the heavy oak door. She shrugged her shoulders impatiently. Time enough to worry about servants and how she would escape when the deed was done. In her present mood a few years in prison seemed a small price to pay for the satisfaction of wounding Lord Carrisford.

She searched frantically through the plaited-straw case for a night-dress and pulled the first one she found ruthlessly over her tumbled curls. The smell of stale perfume conveniently masked the lingering odour of gunpowder which clung to her finger-tips. She pushed the portmanteau and the cloak-bag back under the bed, and stuffed the straw basket along side them. She checked to make sure that the firing mechanism on both pistols was safely locked, then tucked the weapons among the fluffed-up covers. Panting with triumph, she stopped her preparations and stared into the long cheval glass swinging by the side of the dressing-table.

She scarcely recognised the wild creature who stared back at her from its depths. She ran a hand through her tangled mass of hair and touched her finger-tips to her burning cheeks. Her brown eyes smouldered with rage, and angry color stood out against the natural pallor of her complexion. Even through the cambric of her bed-gown she could see the swift rise and fall of her breasts as she struggled to regain control of her breathing. She stared again, frightened by the unexpected passion that shimmered around her like an aura. She turned away quickly and ran to bed, lying back against the pillows in a parody of relaxation. She clenched her hand round the loaded pistol and concealed it beneath the layers of silken coverings. The cool weight of iron felt gratifyingly solid against the feverish heat of her body.

She could not tell how long she waited to hear the sound of Lord Carrisford's footsteps. She seemed to be scarcely breathing as she heard his hand upon the door, then the slight exclamation as he tried to turn the handle. Finally, she heard the grinding of a key in the lock.

When Lord Carrisford entered the room she suspected immediately that he had been drinking. His eyes glittered in the firelight, and it seemed to her that he swayed slightly as he walked across the room. He bowed to her, however, with his habitual, mocking courtesy.

'I regret that the door was locked. It was not barred upon my instructions.'

She did not believe him, of course, but she still smiled at him coquettishly. 'La, sir, I had not observed that it was. I have had no reason to try and leave the room.'

'Have you not?' He seemed to consider her answer, then paced restlessly two or three times around the room. 'Would you care for some champagne? It would be appropriate to celebrate, I trust.'

'Oh no, my lord! Do not call back the servants!' She spoke too vehemently and smiled nervously in an effort to cover up her mistake. 'You have already kept me waiting too long, my lord. What need have we for champagne?'

He tossed his jacket on to the chair and tugged at the folds of his cravat. 'I'm flattered by your eagerness, my dear,' he said sardonically. 'What has happened between our parting this afternoon and my arrival this evening to cause such a marvellous change?'

She racked her brains for a suitable response. It was difficult to think coherently when his body seemed to loom very large in the confinement of her room. She had never before seen a gentleman without his coat on, and she was forced to avert her eyes from the fascinating spectacle of Lord Carrisford unlacing the strings of his undershirt. 'It has been lonely,' she said at last. 'And your servants are not very friendly.'

He walked casually towards the bed, and she could see now that lines of fatigue were etched around his mouth. The slight sway of his movements was caused, perhaps, as much by tiredness as by alcohol. He smiled at her quite kindly.

'You must not mind the servants, Caroline. They are inherited from my father, a worthy man who undoubtedly missed his calling. He would have made an excellent pastor in one of America's most Puritan colonies. There is nothing personal in the attitude of the servants towards you. Indeed, they are probably more disapproving of me than they are of you. Atkins, the butler, is a follower of the Wesley brothers, and he has been known to quote lengthy extracts from the Psalms at me when I come home too much under the weather.' He stood at the end of the bed and looked at her with eyes darkened by a sudden flare of passion. 'God, Caroline, but you're a beautiful woman.'

As if in a nightmare, she sensed him walking closer to her, leaning over the side of the bed, reaching out to pull her into his arms. Just for a moment, as he started to kiss her, she felt paralysed with shock then, to her horror, her lips melted under the pressure of his kiss and a wild flicker of delight flamed through her body. With a desperate effort she wrenched herself out of his arms and pulled out the pistol from its hiding-place under the covers.

'Do not touch me, my lord,' she gasped. 'I am going to shoot you in payment for the humiliations you have inflicted upon me.'

He fell back from the bed in silent amazement, started to laugh, then stared at her with sudden incredulity. 'By heaven, I do believe you are serious.'

Caroline steadied the weapon in both hands. 'Of course I am serious,' she said. 'I am going to shoot you now. Hold still, or I cannot guarantee to hit only your shoulder.'

The silence in the darkened room lengthened oppressively. Caroline's hands trembled around the gun, her arms felt dragged down by its weight. She stared into Lord Carrisford's saturnine features, willing her fingers to pull the trigger. At last, the gun fell out of her hands.

'I can't,' she whispered. 'Oh, how I hate myself, but I cannot do it.'

Lord Carrisford approached the bed with evident caution. 'Then do you think I might take charge of the weapon? Since you have decided against murdering me, I should hate either of us to be the victim of an accident.'

Meekly, she handed him the pistol. 'Oh, why did I not shoot you when you first came into the room? Why am I such a *coward?*'

'Let us not take time to analyse your charitable motives just at the moment. I am quite content merely to be grateful.' Lord

Carrisford stood up from the bed and dragged over a chair, placing it in such a way that he could see Caroline quite plainly from where he sat. It did not require a very close scrutiny to see that her face was deathly pale, and her eyes full of tears.

'Do you have any more surprises in store for me?' he asked her. 'Any bows and arrows under the pillow, or perhaps a cudgel up the sleeve of your night-gown?'

'There is another pistol, my lord, but it is not loaded.'

'Nevertheless, perhaps we should return both guns to their case. I have a constitutional dislike of discussing sensitive subjects when there are weapons to hand.' He smiled. 'Diplomats, you know, are trained to win their arguments with words.'

'Words have not so far achieved very much between us, my lord. I could not persuade you to take my refusals seriously.'

He looked at her consideringly, with no hint of either mockery or cruelty in his expression. 'I cannot, in all honesty, accept the blame for what has happened between us. But I see now that there have been grave misunderstandings.' A wry smile twisted his mouth.

'You will note that I am a man of acute

perceptions. It does not take more than a loaded pistol pointed at my heart before I am able to understand every hint you care to give me.'

She laughed a little shakily. 'At least it was not necessary to pull the trigger!' She rubbed a hand across her eyes. 'Short of turning one of those pistols upon myself, my lord, I cannot think what I should do next. My nervous system must be less robust than I thought, for I'm afraid the events of the past week seem to have robbed me of all capacity for sensible planning.'

Lord Carrisford spoke dryly. 'I take it that a career as my mistress is definitely not part of your plans for the future?'

'It never was, my lord. I am sorry that I led you to suppose otherwise. The Comtesse was eager for me to accept your offer, but I always intended to be firm in my refusal. Unfortunately, my temper is easily aroused, and your offer of that wretched diamond necklace was fatal to my self-control. Your manners, my lord, are a mite overbearing, and I'm afraid that my temper and your manners have proved a fatal combination.'

'But let us be quite clear upon certain matters, Caroline. I would like to know exactly how this situation was allowed to arise between us. The Comtesse made no difficulties whatsoever about my proposals. Indeed, she was flattering in the warmth of her approval. You yourself came to these apartments quite willingly. I did not have to abduct you, my dear.'

She could not find any reasonable explanation for her own actions, so she tried to excuse her stepmother. 'The Comtesse has not been a cruel guardian, my lord, but for some reason she has suddenly become concerned about my future. Perhaps she was startled to discover that I had reached the advanced age of five-and-twenty without managing to marry myself off.'

'I would not have thought you lacked for suitors. Your appearance is not precisely repulsive.'

Caroline smiled wryly. 'My pockets, however, present a less pleasing appearance. And the Comtesse is justified in pointing out that since I work in a gaming-house it is illogical of me to expect to receive offers of marriage.'

'The Comtesse's motives are explained,' said Lord Carrisford. 'But why did you agree to come here?'

Caroline subsided into an embarrassed silence. She had no wish to describe the pressure that Comtesse had applied in order to achieve her own ends. 'My stepmother is not always an easy person to resist,' she said at last. 'I planned to go to my cousins in Harrogate, but when I attempted to leave here this evening I found my door was locked. I became so angry when I discovered that I had been locked in that I wanted to exact some sort of revenge upon you.'

'In truth, Caroline, the locked door was not my idea. The servants have been with our family for a long time and sometimes show their loyalty in strange ways.' Lord Carrisford got up from his chair and strolled over to the fireplace where he appeared to become absorbed in contemplation of his finger-nails.

'I suppose your reasons for coming here, instead of going straight to Harrogate, had nothing to do with the money which was paid into your bank account earlier this week?'

Caroline flushed. 'No, my lord. If you speak to your bankers tomorrow you will find that money you made over to me was returned the same day to you.' She dropped her eyes as she continued speaking, unable to meet his scrutiny. 'I did plan to pawn The diamond necklace. Your manner of giving it to me . . . what you said . . . In short, I can't pretend to be guiltless in this whole affair.'

'If that is your only guilt, then I don't think your conscience need trouble you unduly. I must ask about your stepbrother, Caroline. What part did his affairs play in your decision to enter my household?'

'No part, my lord.' As always she leapt to the defence of her stepbrother, realising too late that the vehemence of her reply rendered it suspect. She tried to modify the effect of her response. 'Philippe didn't even know that I was coming here,' she said.

She was not sure if Lord Carrisford accepted her statement, but he did not press her further. He pulled open the doors of a small cupboard, revealing a shelf that held a decanter of wine and several silver goblets. He drank two generous measures of wine in quick succession before glancing back at Caroline. He saw that she was still huddled primly beneath the covers of the bed and gave her a smile that was full of undeniable charm.

'I must say that we are in the devil of a mess, my dear, and I do not immediately see how we are to come clear. There are complications I have not yet discussed with

97

you; reasons why I particularly wished to have you living with me.' He smiled at her again. 'Other than those entrancing brown eyes, of course.'

Caroline leaned forward eagerly. 'My lord, if you will but consent to help me there will not be the least problem in the world. If you would purchase me a ticket on the stage to Harrogate I need ask nothing further from you. I would repay the loan as soon as I started work, my lord. I could send you the whole sum within a year, for I am sure there would be no difficulty in finding employment in Harrogate. My father's cousins will be there to vouch for the respectability of my background.' She firmly put aside all memory of the wearing rounds of the London employment agencies, none of which had resulted in a job. 'Harrogate is a busy watering-place with many opportunities for finding work. The activities of a girl from a London gaming-house will never have been reported in a spot so far removed from the London scene.'

'I daresay you could find work,' said Lord Carrisford. 'But surely, Caroline, you cannot wish to eke out your life in the company of crotchety old ladies?'

'I must endeavour to become used to the idea, however, and perhaps it will not be as difficult as you expect.' Caroline's attempt at laughter was somewhat forced. 'Who knows what excitements may wait for me in Harrogate? I daresay there are some elderly ladies who lead a life that is gay to the point of dissipation.'

'Then what on earth would they be doing in a watering-place hidden in the wilds of Yorkshire?' asked Lord Carrisford. He stood up from the chair and paced restlessly around the room.

'I must think for a moment, Caroline. There are factors I must consider.' His eyes gleamed with sudden amusement. 'I have a suggestion to make to you, but I must choose my words carefully. Having narrowly escaped a bullet in the shoulder, I don't now wish to run the danger of a sharp blow to the head if I should happen to phrase my request tactlessly.'

'I have indulged in sufficient fits of freakish temper for the time being,' said Caroline ruefully. 'I am concentrating on practising the feminine virtues of modesty and restraint.'

Lord Carrisford smiled. 'Your looks are against you, my dear. Be you never so modest and restrained, those ridiculous curls are bound to speak against you.'

Caroline touched her hair self-consciously, and Lord Carrrisford walked over to the fire with a sudden abrupt movement. He shrugged his shoulders back into his shirt and looked into the mirror with apparent concentration as he reknotted his muslin cravat. 'Do you have a dressing-gown?' he asked. 'I will bring it to you if you have, then we may discuss the matter I have in mind.' He smiled slightly. 'It will be better, I think, if we are both more or less dressed before I make my suggestion.'

Caroline was amused. 'You feel that wearing a dressing-gown will make matters right between us, my lord?'

'No. But it may prevent them going even more disastrously awry,' he said curtly. He was now once again fully clothed and looking remarkably elegant for a man dressed without the services of his valet. Caroline felt a tightening of the muscles in her stomach and turned away hastily.

'There are dressing-gowns in that cupboard, my lord.'

'Very good. Now I can explain some of my problems to you.'

Chapter Seven

'YOU were angry with me earlier this afternoon,' said Lord Carrisford as Caroline settled herself in the chair across the hearth from his own. 'You had some justification, because I deliberately tried to provoke your stepbrother to anger. I even hoped that you yourself might be betrayed into some indiscreet revelations.'

He ignored Caroline's exclamation and continued quickly. 'I had good reason to believe that young de la Rivière could help me solve some problems that have been troubling our government recently. *That* is why I made an offer for you to the Comtesse. I thought that if I took over Philippe's reputed mistress, I might find out some interesting facts about his background.'

'Once you discovered that I was merely Philippe's stepsister I'm surprised that you did not bundle me out of Carrisford House before nightfall.'

'You cannot have looked in a mirror recently, my dear. My pursuit of your favours was not undertaken *entirely* in the line of duty.'

Caroline made haste to turn the subject of the conversation. 'In what way could Philippe help you solve a British government problem?'

Lord Carrisford pushed back his chair and looked uncomfortably at Caroline. 'I suppose the Comtesse de la Rivière never mentioned the existence of another son to you? Older than Philippe and thus fully entitled, even under the old laws of France, to claim the lands and estates of the de la Rivière family?'

Caroline stared at him in amazement. 'The Comtesse has never mentioned any other children,' she said firmly. 'And even if she had, what could that possibly have to do with the British government and its problems?'

Lord Carrisford looked at her steadily. 'There are some facts, Caroline, that I am not at liberty to disclose. But do you wish to hear as much of the story as I can tell you? Will you consider helping me?'

She touched her hands to her burning cheeks. 'Since this matter concerns my stepbrother and his mother I very much want to hear what you have to say, my lord.'

'I came to your stepmother's club because of information I was given in Spain,' said

Lord Carrisford. 'My position in the Peninsula was such that I was often approached by the agents of other governments. Among the men who made contact with me was a young French soldier who called himself the Count de la Rivière.' He ignored Caroline's gasp of denial and continued his restless pacing of the bedroom. 'The Count provided me with the information I needed, valuable military information about Napoleon's overall campaign plans. Without his intervention, and the details he gave to me, I am doubtful if we could have persuaded the Prince Regent of Portugal to stand firm in his support of our cause.' He smiled ruefully. 'The Prince is hardly a man of supreme personal courage, and most of his advisors can hardly wait to join the exiled King in Brazil.'

'This man . . . this Count . . . You believe he is actually a Royalist agent, although he is officially working on Bonaparte's personal staff?'

'I wish I knew. Certainly the information he gave us on this occasion worked against Napoleon's immediate interests. However, Napoleon is a master strategist. He is perfectly prepared to sacrifice the occasional battle so long as he can be sure of winning the war. The Count de la Rivière, if he is the Count, is undoubtedly an agent. The question I cannot answer is whether he is an agent working for the Bourbons, or for Napoleon, or merely for himself.'

'But why should you place any reliance upon his word when we know for a fact that he is an impostor? Philippe is the Comte de la Rivière, attested to by his mother. Surely even you agree that the Comtesse must know her own son?'

'During my two clandestine meetings with Count André de la Rivière, he told me something of his own past history. You will understand that we were meeting behind hedgerows between the battle lines and the conditions were hardly conductive to a lengthy exchange of confidences. But I gathered that he had been brought up from boyhood by a family of lawyers with Republican sympathies. He had no reason to rebel against their support of the Republic or their espousal of Bonaparte's cause. When he came of age, his guardians took him for a visit to the de la Rivière estates in Burgundy and told him that he was the heir both to the title and to these lands. The visit to these estates touched some chord, and for the first time he developed a sympathy for the plight of the former aristoc-racy. He concealed these new sympathies from his guardians, however, and decided that he would secretly offer his aid to the Royalist cause. His position as a young of-ficer on Napoleon's personal staff gave him a unique opportunity to aid the Royalist cause, and thus the British campaign, if he truly wished to do so.'

Caroline struggled to sort out her bewil-dered thoughts. 'But if he is heir to the Rivière estates he must be the Comtesse's son. Why in the world would she wish to conceal the fact of his existence? If he is her son, and therefore brother to Philippe, there can be no reason for her to ignore his just claims to the Rivière inheritance.'

'I did not say that this man *was* the true Comte de la Rivière, Caroline. I said merely that he claimed to be so. However, the re-semblance of this young man to Philippe de la Rivière is startling and lends credence to his claims. He insists, you see, that until he returned to the family estates in Burgundy he had no idea that his mother had escaped the executions meted out to his father and so many other Royalist leaders. He was amazed to discover from peasants on the estate that his mother had not only escaped to England, but had taken her four-year-old son with her. He learned for the first time that he might have a younger brother, Philippe de la Rivière.'

Caroline's face showed her dismay. 'The Comtesse is such a devoted mother. I cannot believe that she would have left behind one of her sons, whatever the circumstances. And then you are asking me to believe that she has kept Philippe in ignorance of his brother's existence, and ignorant of his superior claim to the Rivière estate. It is just not possible, my lord.'

'It is possible that the Comtesse is misinformed, Caroline. Her motives may not be malicious. The man I met claims he was left entirely in his father's hands. The parents decided that they would double their chances for escape if each planned separately and each was responsible for only one of the children. The Comtesse was successful in her plans but, as far as she knew, the Comte had failed. Undoubtedly she found it easier not to mention the son she had lost. Why burden Philippe with memories of his brother? He already had more than enough sadness to bear. You have an expressive face, Caroline, and I can see that what I have told you bears out whatever you know of the Comtesse's story. Am I not right?'

She could not bear to acknowledge just how plausible Count André's story was beginning to sound. When had Philippe first learned of the possible existence of a brother who might be the true heir to the Rivière estate? She still hoped to prove that Lord Carrisford had been misinformed. 'How did your supposed Count explain his escape from the Terror?' she asked.

'The treacherous servant who betrayed the old Comte could not bring himself to deliver a seven-year-old child into the lap of the guillotine. He rescued the young heir and boarded him secretly with a distant branch of the Rivière family.' Lord Carrisford shrugged eloquently. 'For what it's worth, there is no doubt that Napoleon's government considers André to be the true count, and the heir to the Rivière estate. He is also considered a valuable supporter of their cause.'

'How can you trust a man who takes favours from the Bonapartist government and then claims to support the Royalists?'

Lord Carrisford answered her quietly. 'Our loyalties are not always decided as easily as we would wish. Who is to say which is the greater treason? To support Bona- parte or to fight him?' He sighed. 'It is fash- ionable in England to pretend that Napoleon is a monster. If we call him a monster, it is easier for us to forget that he is a very great man.'

'Those are strange sentiments, my lord, for a man who was doubting my own loy- alties not very many hours ago.'

'The trouble with diplomacy as a profes- sion is that it either encourages us to become expert liars or we develop an unfortunate capacity for seeing the other man's point of view. I have frequently noticed, in recent months, that my vision is expanding to the point where it is in danger of becoming cir- cular.'

'And now you wish me to jump on your merry-go-round, my lord.' Caroline found it easier to pour scorn upon Lord Carrisford than to think profoundly concerning the worrying information she had just been given. 'You still have not even begun to explain how I am to help you in the unrav- elling of this mystery. In fact, the more I hear the less I understand how this purely family matter can be of any interest to you or to our government. Providing that the information which Count André sends is accurate, what does it matter whether or not he is the elder son of the Comtesse de la Rivière? Even if he is a total impostor, how can it affect the value of his information?'

'To a certain extent, you are correct. But Count André has now approached one of my subordinates with information which is so startling, and so much contrary to all that we have learned from other sources, that the Prime Minister is in a quandary as to how we should proceed. He can ignore the information entirely, in which case our armies in Spain may find themselves making most costly blunders, or we can accept his information as correct. If we decide to accept Count André's information, Viscount Wellington will make crucial changes in his strategy for the battles now in preparation in the Peninsula. So you see, we are anxious to ascertain how much reliance we may place upon Count André's words.'

'And you feel that to establish the truth of his claims in regard to the Rivière estate somehow enhances the value of his other information? I do not see much connection, my lord. The Rivière estates are valuable, and he may well be dishonest in making his claims to those lands even if the rest of his information is entirely accurate.'

'If we knew that Count André was indeed the legitimate descendant of a noble family with a history of service to the Bourbon crown, it would tend to give more weight to his statement that he no longer supports Napoleon Bonaparte. It would not, of course, clinch the matter one way or another. The Marquis de Lafayette, to cite but one example, comes from one of the most distinguished Royalist families in France, but he was a leader of the early reform movements. Family heritage is not everything, and the legitimacy of Count André's claim is not my primary interest in this matter. The Count had given us a more certain method of testing his loyalty to the Royalist cause and his willingness to aid the British government. He has given us the name of a leading Bonapartist sympathiser in this country. I have already made contact with some minor French agents, and it seems possible that Count André's information is correct. If it is, then our government will be able to accept Count André's other information with far greater confidence. After all, it is no small thing to betray the name of the most important Bonapartist agent working in London.'

Caroline turned pale. 'Am I to be told

who this mysterious and powerful French agent is, my lord?'

Lord Carrisford looked at her consideringly. 'You suspect already, I think. It is Philippe de la Rivière.'

'No, my lord!' The protest was instinctive. 'It cannot be Philippe! He has not the remotest interest in politics. He cares nothing for the battles that wage between France and England.'

'Have you never found such indifference strange?' asked Lord Carrrisford. 'After all, one would imagine your stepbrother would have an acute interest in the outcome of events in France. His father was seigneur over a large stretch of prosperous Burgundy land, while he is an assistant in his mother's gaming-house. Upon reflection, do you not find political indifference from such a young man curious?'

Caroline hesitated on the brink of a vehement denial, but in the end honesty forced her to confess how little she had ever stopped to consider Philippe's political views.

'I am accustomed to thinking of Philippe as a boy, scarcely over the threshold of manhood. I have made no effort to share his serious thoughts and aspirations.'

She tried to judge Philippe's political thoughts objectively. It was true he resented his position at the gaming-house. He disliked being poor and handled his financial affairs irresponsibly. But that need not mean he was prepared to work secretly for the success of a régime that was anathema to the mother whom he loved. Caroline shook her head.

'You are wrong, my lord. You will find out that Philippe is what he appears on the surface. A restless young man who has not yet found his precise niche in life.'

'In that case you should be anxious to help me prove his innocence,' said Lord Carrisford. 'Doubts have been raised about Philippe's integrity. Surely you wish to clear up the slur cast upon his name?'

'Of course I do. But how can I help?'

Lord Carrisford regarded her in tense silence. 'I have already told you that I went to the Comtesse's house simply to observe Philippe and to meet you. I wanted to assess my chances of making you my mistress, because I could think of no other method of penetrating Philippe's guard so quickly.' He paused and looked away from her when he spoke again. 'I still want you to stay in my house,' he said. 'I want you to pretend to be my mistress even though I accept it will only be a pretence. Originally I had hoped to throw Philippe off balance by snatching his mistress and confidante from under his nose. Now I wish to achieve the same result by appearing to seduce his stepsister.'

When she said nothing, but simply stared at him in stony silence, he added stiltedly. 'You have my word that my attentions will cease the moment we walk through the front door of my house.'

For a moment after he finished speaking, Caroline continued to sit in silence, too stunned to speak. She realised at last that he was serious in making his outrageous suggestion, and she got to her feet, drawing her robe tightly around her.

'My lord, I think you have taken leave of your senses. Would you care to explain to me just why you think this scandalous pretence is necessary?'

Lord Carrisford pushed her back into the seat with an impatient exclamation. 'Do sit down, Caroline. Where are you planning to go at three in the morning? The pretence is necessary because I have no time to organise more subtle stratagems. Time is of the essence in this matter. The British government *must* know which sources of intelligence to believe. I need intimate access to Philippe and his circle of acquaintance without delay.'

'I should think he is more likely to run his sword through your heart than to admit you into the circle of his acquaintance. He cherishes a high opinion of my honour.'

'If he is London's leading French agent he will soon be aware of my activities in the Peninsula and I think the defence of your virtue will be the least of his worries.'

Caroline found it absurd to picture Philippe in the rôle of a leading government agent. So absurd, in fact, that she could not concentrate her arguments on rebutting Lord Carrisford's words.

'I don't suppose you are worried by the fact that I shall lose the remaining shreds of my reputation?' she said angrily.

'On the contrary, I have given some thought to that problem. If you agree to take part in my scheme I shall make some financial provision for your future. I will settle a thousand pounds upon you, thus providing a dowry for you to take to those respectable Harrogate cousins.'

Caroline thought wistfully of a thousand pounds and what it might mean for her future. 'My lord, I cannot . . . must not . . .

agree to your plan. It would be wrong to accept your money, and I couldn't play the rôle of your mistress with any conviction.' She permitted herself a small smile. 'I lack experience.'

'You don't have to act very convincingly, Caroline. With your looks, I have merely to sigh languidly while staring into your beautiful eyes and all of London will know that I am enslaved.'

She blushed. 'You are nonsensical, my lord.' He seemed unmoved by this remark, so she repeated her somewhat uncertain denial. 'I could not do it. I *ought* not to do it.'

'Your stepbrother's future lies in your hands. If he is innocent, don't you wish to prove it as soon as possible? If he is guilty, don't you wish to know in time to cushion the blow for your stepmother?'

She felt her powers of resistance weakening in the face of such arguments. She pressed her fingers to her aching temples, trying to prod herself into logical thought, but it was no use. Lord Carrisford's compelling gaze seemed to mesmerise her into obedience. She could scarcely believe it, when she heard her own voice accepting the rôle he was thrusting upon her.

'Very well, my lord, you have won the battle. I will play the part of your mistress. We both know that my reputation is already ruined beyond repair, so it cannot matter if we flaunt the tatters around town for a few days.'

Lord Carrisford bowed deeply. It was impossible to judge his reaction to her submission, since his expression remained inscrutable. 'I am grateful to you, Caroline, and I shall endeavour to see that you do not regret your decision.' He turned at the door, his eyes glinting in the firelight. 'I shall leave instructions with the servants that you are not to be disturbed tomorrow morning.' She thought she detected a faint smile at the corner of his mouth. 'They will, in any case, expect you to be exhausted.'

Chapter Eight

BY the third morning of her stay at Carrisford House Caroline decided to abandon her feeble attempts at self-deception. It was foolish to pretend that she planned to flee to Harrogate, when several perfectly good opportunities for escape had already come and passed by deliberately unheeded. Although she was dismayed at the ease with which she had fallen into the rôle of Lord Carrisford's mistress, an essential integrity prevented her from concealing the frank pleasure she derived from his company. She knew that even the most liberal of her parents' friends would be appalled at the scandalous part she had agreed to play. What those same upright citizens would think of her *pleasure* in such a life did not bear contemplating.

On the whole, Caroline decided, it was advisable to avoid thinking as much as possible, and she tried to convince herself during the inevitable moments of doubt that it was best simply to live from moment to moment. She made a great effort to reflect as little as possible either on the future or on the past. Since she had already resigned herself to the fact that there was little likelihood of her crossing the threshold of any respectable household ever again, it was surprisingly easy simply to enjoy the pleasures of the present. Sometimes she found herself slipping into a foolish daydream in which she remained at Carrisford House for ever, but for the most part she managed to keep her feet firmly planted on Lord Carrisford's exquisitely polished floors.

Despite the startling changes in her circumstances, and the occasional foolish daydream, Caroline prided herself upon retaining most of her store of common sense. She therefore considered Fate to have dealt her an unkind blow when it became apparent that her stay with Lord Carrisford was destined to be longer than either of them had originally anticipated. By some capricious quirk of destiny, her stepbrother decided to leave London on the very day that Caroline commenced her masquerade. The message announcing his departure was conveyed first to the Comtesse's house and then carried round to Caroline, too late for her to prevent Philippe from leaving.

The note, typical of Philippe's extravagant style, contained many protestations of undying devotion but remarkably few facts as to where he was actually going. He was leaving London, he wrote, 'to join my friends for the races.' It was left to Caroline's imagination to supply the names of the friends and the location of the races.

Upon receiving the delayed message, Caroline hastened to convey the contents of the note to Lord Carrisford. She did not like to ask herself why the mere thought of a brief interview with her employer was sufficient to set her heart beating more swiftly, and she resolutely ignored the quick colour that suffused her cheeks as she hastened to twitch her gown into place in front of the mirror. She tucked a stray curl back behind the blue velvet ribbon adorning her hair, and smoothed down the spotless muslin of her morning-gown. Then she went quickly down the private staircase, familiar now after two days in Carrisford House, and knocked on the library door.

Lord Carrisford was reading a document culled from a pile of papers scattered over his desk when Caroline answered his command to enter, but he pushed this aside and stood up as soon as she came into the room. He smiled at her, and Caroline gulped awkwardly. She always felt uncomfortable in the face of Lord Carrisford's casual gestures of friendship. She thrust Philippe's note into his hand.

'Only see what my stepbrother has written, my lord,' she said hurriedly. 'Are you not frustrated at this delay in our plans? Is it not annoying that Philippe should have chosen this—of all the weeks in the year—to disappear with his cronies?'

Lord Carrisford looked amused. 'I would

not have said annoying, Caroline. Perhaps "convenient" would be a better word.'

'Convenient! Convenient for whom? Certainly not for me. I swear that if your housekeeper casts even one more freezing look in my direction when she brings up the morning chocolate, I shall turn into an icicle. One day soon, you will come down to breakfast, my lord, and find me a frozen statue seated across the table.'

He laughed. 'I must rely upon your choleric temperament, my dear, to avoid such a horrible possibility. I am confident that your warm blood will ward off the effects of Bessie's hostile stares. Remember that I have endured similar scowls for years, and I stand before you still warm with life.'

Just in time Caroline recalled the original point of her question. 'You have not yet told me who will find Philippe's absence convenient, my lord.'

'I myself, naturally, since it give me several days in which to enjoy all the charm of your—er—conversation. And Philippe too, perhaps? I leave you to judge whether or not your brother might find it convenient to be away from town just at the moment.'

All Caroline's endeavours to elicit a more satisfactory response proved quite unavailing, so she had, perforce, to resign herself to the prospect of several extra days in a rôle that should have offended every principle carefully instilled by the late, highly virtuous, Mrs Adams.

Unfortunately, since self-deception was not one of Caroline's well-developed attributes, she could not conceal from herself the lamentable truth that her position in Lord Carrisford's household exactly suited her temperament. His lively intelligence matched her own, and his experience was so much broader that she was able to revel in the delights of a companionship more stimulating than any she had previously known. His taste in entertainment tallied precisely with her own, and she was a happy witness to more plays and concerts during the first week in his house than in the whole of the last year spent working for the Comtesse.

Ironically, she was finding it increasingly necessary to warn herself against a dangerous awareness of his attractions. As the days passed he seemed to become less and less aware of her as a woman, while she became more and more aware of him as a man. By the end of the week Lord Carrisford's failure to try to seduce her had been added to

Caroline's lengthening list of topics not to be thought about.

In view of her increasingly errant thoughts, she waited with mounting anxiety to hear that Philippe had returned to town. The tantalising pleasures of her relationship with Lord Carrisford had to be brought to a swift end if she was to save herself from a reckless decision to toss her bonnet over the windmill and count all well lost for love. There was, therefore, no denying the relief that flooded through her when Lord Carrisford came into her bedroom one morning with the news that Philippe was back in London, after an absence of almost ten days.

Lord Carrisford made his announcement before dropping casually into the room's most comfortable armchair, propping his feet on the side of the fender with the relaxed air of a man planning to stay. Caroline was too pleased to learn that Philippe was back in town to wonder how Lord Carrisford had heard of his arrival.

'You appear very pleased that your job of work can now commence,' said Lord Carrisford. 'I take it that you have been finding our time together less than enjoyable?'

Caroline could barely restrain herself

from blurting out the truth and confessing how dreary the hours seemed when they were apart, but she managed a nonchalant shrug of the shoulders. 'It is better if we disprove the accusations against my step-brother as soon as possible. After all, we are both anxious to return to the natural course of our own lives. You cannot wish me to be here any more than I wish to re-main.'

'Would living with me permanently be so very bad?' asked Lord Carrisford.

Caroline drew in a sharp breath. How easy it would be to admit that such a life would be heaven. 'It would be unbearable, my lord,' she said brusquely.

Lord Carrisford finally looked up from the fire.

'It is of no consequence. My question was merely rhetorical, since you are quite un-suited to the rôle of my mistress.' He paused for a few moments, and when he spoke again his voice was light and impersonally friendly. 'I understand that your step-brother goes to Covent Garden theatre to-night. Will you join me at the same play?'

'Of course. You know how much I enjoy the theatre.'

He looked at her intently, and then said

gently, 'Your brother will be very displeased, my dear. He will see us alone in
my private box, and he will not be able to
misunderstand the situation. It is a very
public declaration of your rôle in my life.'

She would not let him see how she
shrank from the prospect. 'We have been
to the theatre before, my lord. How will
this be any different except that Philippe is
to be there?' Her voice was not quite as
carefree as she had hoped to make it.

He looked away. 'So far I have been at
pains to shield you from the undesirable
attentions of our acquaintances,' he said. 'I
remembered how distressed you were by
that encounter with Sir Geoffrey Hume, and
I have taken steps to see that such meetings
were not repeated. But tonight I no longer
wish to protect you. I wish to flaunt your
rôle before the public eye. Time presses,
and I need to reach some decisions.'

Caroline thought of the two footmen who
had been permanently stationed outside
their box on previous visits to the play, and
the elderly maidservant who had sat primly
behind her throughout the long performances. Now she realised why their outings
had been so free of the painful snubs she
had steeled herself to encounter. She looked

up at Lord Carrisford, quailing inwardly at the closed expression that shuttered his features. She could no longer disguise the tremor in her voice.

'How am I to be flaunted, my lord?' she asked. 'What do you mean exactly?'

He got up without saying anything and strode over to the dressing-room. She saw him unlock one of the drawers in a small writing-desk, and watched in mesmerised silence as he pulled out a massive leather jewel-case. He seemed almost angry as he came back into the bedroom and pushed the case towards Caroline.

'Open it,' he commanded harshly. 'I want you to wear those tonight.'

Carefully she lifted the black padded lid and gasped at the blaze of colour which met her eyes. Sapphires, rubies and emeralds blinked at the centre of diamond clusters arranged to resemble bouquets of flowers. Gingerly she lifted up a coil of stones and saw that they were fashioned into a shimmering necklace. A bracelet and broach remained on the bed of velvet. She stared at Lord Carrisford in silent horror, but he ignored her unspoken plea and once more crossed over the room with grim purposefulness.

'Here,' he said, handing her another box. 'Here is the matching tiara.'

It was too much. Caroline glanced at the crown of multi-coloured jewels, surely elaborate enough to have adorned the head of an Empress, and an hysterical laugh punctured the silence of the room. Almost immediately, the laughter turned to panic. 'My lord,' she whispered, 'I cannot wear such jewels. They are . . . they are . . .' Words failed her, and she ended lamely, 'Besides, they must be worth a King's ransom. I should be terrified to step outside the door.'

'If you are worried about losing them, perhaps I can reassure you by pointing out that the jewels are paste. The settings are of real gold because that is hard to counterfeit in such delicate workmanship, but the stones are imitations. Cleverly done, but intrinsically worthless, I assure you.'

'But do you think all the footpads will know that?' asked Caroline shakily.

Lord Carrisford smiled. 'I shall be there to take care of you. So if that is your only objection, we may consider the matter settled.'

'Of course it is not my only objection,' said Caroline. 'If I wear such an incredibly vulgar display, everyone will think . . . will think . . .'

'Exactly what they are supposed to think,' said Lord Carrisford dryly. 'You may perhaps remember that the whole purpose of this exercise is to convince Philippe—and his French associates if he has any around him at the theatre—that I have finally gone crazy over a woman. A woman, moreover, who is rather closely involved with some of the main protagonists in one of their current dramas.' He looked at her reflectively. 'It is not at all hard to imagine a man losing his head over somebody who looks as you do. And since I am known to possess a large fortune, we must deck you out accordingly. I cannot send you out in a debutante's dress and a string of pearls.'

Caroline thrust the jewels back into the box and stood up abruptly. 'You are probably right, my lord.' She lifted her head up higher and turned away from the lighted window so that he would not see that her hands were shaking. 'The sooner this is begun, the sooner it will be over. I shall wear the jewels tonight and a gown which will complement their effect. What are you hoping for, my lord? That Philippe will take

127

one look at me, then run over to our box proclaiming that he is in league with Napoleon Bonaparte? All this, of course, before he runs a sword through your heart, which I do not doubt he will attempt to do.'

'Fashion is on my side, my dear. I do not think Philippe will be wearing a sword, and I trust wiser counsels will prevail before he has time to dash out and find one.'

She tried to smile, but her face was white and her lips were clenched tightly together to stop her teeth from chattering. With an impatient exclamation, Lord Carrisford walked over to the dressing-table where she was standing and pulled her back towards the windows. He searched her face in the sunlight streaming in through the thin curtains and then turned sharply away.

'It is still not too late,' he said. 'It was unwise of me to embroil you in this masquerade. If you wish to be released from your promise. Caroline, I will call upon the services of one of my cousins to offer you shelter until you can journey to Harrogate. I will find you respectable employment, never fear.'

She suspected that she ought to accept his offer, which was more generous than she had any right to expect. But Caroline knew that she could not turn back from the task she had set herself. Philippe was her step-brother, whom she had known and loved for more than eight years. He had crept into her heart as a shy young schoolboy, with gangly arms and a tendency to stutter. She could not thrust his claims aside just for her own convenience. The preposterous claims of the imposter strutting around the battle-fields of the Peninsula must be exposed for the lies they undoubtedly were.

She looked up at Lord Carrisford with more determination than she felt. 'No,' she said quietly. 'I agreed to help you unmask a traitor. I know it will not prove to be my brother and I want to see Philippe's inno-cence publicly acknowledged. How could I run off to Harrogate, knowing of the ac-cusations which threaten Philippe's secu-rity, and my stepmother's peace of mind?'

'The Comtesse does not deserve your consideration,' said Lord Carrisford harshly. 'Does it not matter to you that she was pre-pared to sell your body to the highest bid-der?'

Caroline turned away from the scorn in his expression. 'The Comtesse did not see her actions in that way,' she said quietly. 'I had no hope of marriage and only the slimmest hope of respectable employment. It is very easy for you to condemn my stepmother. You are a nobleman of great wealth. What do you know about life as an *émigré*, scratching for every penny, struggling to maintain some sort of dignified facade, some shreds of personal integrity? The Comtesse is a realist, my lord, and she did not choose to cloak her arrangements for my future in sweet words. What does any women have to sell except her body. Either in marriage or outside of it, the transaction is the same. Only the trappings are different.'

Lord Carrisford looked disconcertingly amused. 'I believe you have been imbibing some very revolutionary French ideas along with the Royalist contents of your stepmother's wine cellars. If my memory serves me correctly—and I am rather noted for the accuracy of my recollections—you struggled to resist my possession of your body with quite dramatic fervour. Why was that, if marriage makes so little difference to the essential transaction?'

Caroline could not begin to answer him, so she took refuge in defiance. 'Just be thankful that I have agreed to participate in your plans.'

Lord Carrisford smiled. 'I *am* thankful. I look for great results from your performance tonight.'

Caroline shuddered inwardly as she thought of the evening ahead of her. Most of all, more than the open scorn of respectable matrons, she dreaded the sly insults and fulsome compliments she would receive from Lord Carrisford's circle of men friends.

'May I have your permission to be alone?' she asked curtly. The conflict of her emotions left her tongue incapable of phrasing the request more politely. 'There is a great deal I must do before this evening if I am to meet with your approval.'

Lord Carrisford flushed with irritation. 'Dammit, Caroline, I'm not your keeper. If you wish to be alone, you have only to say so.'

'I'm sorry, my lord. I keep forgetting that in theory I am a free agent.' She bit her lip on an overwrought gasp of laughter. 'The choice of words was unfortunate, my lord.'

He looked at her darkly. 'Was it, Caroline? Over the past few days I have found myself unable to decide whether you are a French spy, or just an innocent bystander as you pretend. But bear in mind, will you, that I am not easily taken in by a pretty face, and my plans don't require more than a minimum of cooperation from you.'

For a few seconds Caroline stared at him in silence, then the hysterical laughter which these days seemed a constant companion could no longer be contained. 'You suspect *me* of being a French spy, my lord? You imagine that I am the accomplice of my villainous stepbrother?' She tossed her head scornfully. 'What do you think I am doing here? Sending Napoleon transcripts of our dinner menus?'

Lord Carrisford looked at her coldly. 'The French Government would not waste your talents on such a task. There are plenty of out-of-work spies who can be hired to steal documents. But there cannot be many French spies who are able to gain admission to the home of a man such as myself. And certainly none who could hope to captivate me as you are capable of doing.'

'If you think that I have been attempting to captivate you, my lord, then you are sadly out in your judgments. I am staying in your house because I wish to prove my brother's innocence and for no other reason. Now that we have cleared up this area of confusion, perhaps you would leave this room.'

He made a small gesture with his hand, almost as if he would say something further, then his hand fell back to his side and he bowed silently. 'I shall see you this evening, Caroline. Let us hope for both our sakes that events move swiftly from now on.'

Caroline waited until the door shut quietly behind him, and then flung herself on the bed in a storm of weeping. But whether she cried because of Lord Carrisford or because of herself, even she would have been hard pushed to say.

Chapter Nine

LORD Carrisford's barouche joined the long line of carriages waiting to discharge their occupants outside the imposing facade of the new Covent Garden Theatre. The old building had been wiped out by fire in 1808 and now, just over a year later, the remodelled theatre was once more open for business. Mrs Siddons and her brother, John Philip Kemble, commanded the boards with all their former dramatic verve, their skills intensified by a year's enforced absence.

In other circumstances Caroline would

have been delighted at the prospect ahead of her. As it was, she descended from the carriage with all the enthusiasm of a condemned criminal approaching the stake. Lord Carrisford was usually an easy conversationalist despite the unconventional relationship existing between them. Tonight, however, he had remained silent throughout their brief journey to the theatre, leaving Caroline with nothing better to do than worry uselessly about the ordeal she had to face. Now that they had arrived, Lord Carrisford seemed to shrug off his mood of introspection, and he turned to her with an exaggerated display of courteous concern, assisting her over a small puddle and closing the delicate velvet of her evening cape to ensure that no draft could creep through the soft folds. She submitted miserably to his ministrations, managing no more than a watery smile when he bent towards her with a loving glance and hissed angrily in her ear, 'We are supposed To be attending a comedy, you know, not your best friend's funeral.'

With this remark Lord Carrisford's period of silence seemed to be over, for he conducted her into the foyer, pointing out improvements in the design, chatting with all his habitual amiability. His entire object in coming to the theatre appeared to be the procurement of Caroline's entertainment and pleasure.

As they followed one of the footmen to their box, Lord Carrisford maintained his flow of chatter by describing to Caroline the audience riots which had occurred when the new theatre was reopened earlier in the year. Mr Kemble, anxious to recoup some of his financial losses, had increased the prices for admission to the theatre. Not surprisingly, this increase had been extremely unpopular with the poorer members of the public, and they had staged noisy demonstrations during the performances in order to show their disapproval. After several weeks of trying unsuccessfully to make themselves heard over the vigorous foot-stomping and cat-calling of the audience, Kemble and his company acknowledged defeat and returned the prices for the cheaper seats to their original levels. The increased rate for private boxes had, however, remained in force. Lord Carrisford commented dryly that he felt there was some moral to be drawn from this story.

'Of course there is,' said Caroline, who had been listening to Lord Carrisford with less than half her attention. 'If you stamp your feet loudly enough, you get your own way.'

Lord Carrisford laughed. For the first time that evening his manner relaxed into naturalness. 'I trust you are wrong. It seems an undesirable conclusion for us to draw.' He tucked her arm protectively under his own. 'I had better warn you in advance that *I* am entirely immune to stamped feet and temper tantrums of any variety. Having four younger brothers and sisters I have learned that there are only two ways to deal with kicking feet. One is to stop the kicking, by force if necessary, and the other is to ignore it. I disapprove of Mr Kemble's concession, in theory if not in practice.'

They arrived at the padded plush door of their box. They might as well have been walking through a stone tunnel for all Caroline had seen of the wonderous array of gilt and chandeliers. She tried hard to focus her frantic thoughts on Lord Carrisford's conversation. 'Do you have very bad-tempered brothers and sisters, my lord?' she asked distractedly. As soon as the words were uttered, she realised that this was hardly an appropriate question to ask. 'That is to say, I am afraid I was not fully attending.'

'That is obvious,' said Lord Carrisford. He sounded amused, as if his own calm was perfectly restored now that they were actually arrived at the theatre. He signalled to the footman, indicating that he should remain outside the box, and then he escorted Caroline into the richly-carpeted interior.

He waited until she had shed her cloak and was seated upon one of the small gilt armchairs before he even glanced at her pale pink silk evening-gown, allowing his eyes to roam slowly over the gleaming tiara and the opulent falls of jewels at her throat and on both her wrists. Even then he said nothing, but turned to acknowledge the presence of several acquaintances who bowed to him from the stalls. At last, he turned his chair deliberately away from the auditorium. His view of the stage was now obscured, but Caroline's face and figure were directly in his line of sight. Even the most casual observer would realise that Lord Carrisford had no intention of concentrating upon the performance about to be enacted upon the stage. Caroline tried to appear absorbed in contemplation of the painted curtains, draped across the stage. She flicked open her fan and wafted it up and down with jerky movements of the wrist, hoping to cool the flush that remained obstinately fixed on her cheeks. It was ridiculous, immodest even, to imagine that every eye was riveted upon their box.

'You are magnificent tonight,' said Lord Carrisford abruptly. 'Even the vulgarity of those jewels seems acceptable when set against the perfection of your skin. I have never seen hair as flawlessly golden as yours.'

She blushed more deeply at the note of passion in his voice, and for a few moments felt absurdly pleased at his compliments. His next words dispelled the magic.

'Don't turn away,' he said sharply. 'We are being observed from all corners of the theatre. You must smile at me. We are supposed to be *lovers*.'

With the greatest difficulty she forced herself to lean back in her chair and bring her gaze up to meet his own. The flare of emotion which leapt into his eyes struck her with violent force, and she quickly reminded herself that his passion, like her loving smile, was intended only for public show. Unable to cope with the blazing intensity of his look, which although feigned on his part was arousing a tumult of genuine feeling in her, she turned aside to scan the boxes on the other side of the theatre. In one of these, placed almost directly opposite their own, was an elderly woman of fierce aspect and dowdy dress. She was holding forth to the other members of her party in the manner of one accustomed to being listened to without interruption. With a sudden imperious sweep of her shoulders the elderly lady swung round and stared fixedly at Caroline. Her gaze was filled with such evident disdain that Caroline could barely repress a shudder of discomfort. The woman's animosity was tangible, even across the width of the theatre.

Caroline turned back sharply, almost relieved to find Lord Carrisford's eyes still fixed upon her face.

'Who is that lady in the box over there, my lord?'

He raised Caroline's hand to his lips and, with slow deliberation, pressed a kiss on the palm. 'I have had no opportunity to gaze at the other boxes,' he said, and his voice was harsh although his mouth still smiled at her. 'If you remember, we are supposed to be lost in love. Since you are apparently unable to appear even minimally bewitched, my efforts must be redoubled.'

Caroline allowed her hand to remain in

Lord Carrisford's clasp. It was only for appearance sake, she told herself, and not because of the thrilling quiver of sensation that shot through her arm as his lips pressed against the silk of her gloves. 'I am sorry,' she said softly. 'It is merely that she stares at us so.'

'Describe her to me.'

'She is naturally tall, I think, but in addition she holds herself very straight and stiff. She is wearing a grey gown, at least five seasons out of date, with a great cascade of diamonds strung all anyhow about her neck. Her hair is very black, although I imagine she must be more than sixty. *She* looks very fierce, and the rest of her party looks very unhappy.'

Lord Carrisford dropped her hand with unflattering promptness and slewed round to look at the woman Caroline had described. A smile of wry amusement flashed briefly across his face. Slowly he reached for Caroline's hands, and this time clasped both of them within his grasp, at the same time inclining his head to the elderly lady in a tiny, mocking gesture of greeting.

'I thought there could not be more than one person to match your description,' he said as he brought his attention once more back to Caroline. His shoulders were shaken by another brief laugh. 'I have to inform you that you have just made the acquaintance of the Dowager Baroness Carrisford. In other words, my mother.'

'Oh no!' Instinctively Caroline cringed back against the cushions of her chair, seeking to hide herself in the dark shadows at the back of the box.

'Don't be foolish,' commanded Lord Carrisford curtly. 'She cannot acknowledge my presence while you are with me, so you are in no danger of receiving the sharp edge of her tongue. It is I who will have to prepare myself for an onslaught next time we are unfortunate enough to meet.'

Caroline could not feel that this reassurance provided her with much moral comfort, but since the beginning of the play was at the moment heralded on stage she attempted to thrust all thoughts of reality from out of her mind. With two intervals still ahead of her, she felt that the sufferings of the stage heroine could hardly compete with her own woes. The heroine of the play had, after all, merely to escape from the clutches of a murderous and despotic guardian. Caroline needed to escape from the weaknesses of her own heart.

The merits of the play were quite lost upon Caroline, although the famous Mrs Siddons was herself playing the role of the heroine. Mrs Siddons' dramatic gestures and heart-rending cries passed right by Caroline's head, although impressionable females had been known to faint from terror when the actress stormed into one of her theatrical rages. When the curtain fell to mark the arrival of the first interval, Mrs Siddons and her villainous guardian might as well have been reciting the alphabet for all the impact their joint efforts had made on Caroline.

'Do you care for some refreshment?' asked Lord Carrisford politely. 'The sight of so much threatened virtue has left me feeling quite hungry. Shall I send the footman to procure us some food?'

'Oh no, no!' Caroline dreaded leaving the door of their box untended. 'Do not trouble yourself on my account, my lord.'

'Well, perhaps you are right. I have seen Sir Geoffrey Hume in the audience with an—er—former acquaintance of mine. I think they may be coming to visit us. Are you ready to face them, Caroline?' He did not tell her that he had spotted Philippe de la Rivière seated at the back of the stalls.

He did not doubt that they would be receiving a visit from that young man, if not in this interval, then in the next.

She was spared the necessity of answering by the sound of brisk knocking at the door of the box, and almost immediately Sir Geoffrey's jovial features peered round the green velvet livery of the footman. A creamy-complexioned brunette of statuesque proportions leaned familiarly upon his arm.

Lord Carrisford rose to his feet. 'Come in, sir. It is some days since I have had the pleasure of seeing you.'

'Yes . . . er . . . well.' Sir Geoffrey shuffled his feet in embarrassment and kept his eyes carefully averted from the luscious curves of his companion's figure. 'I have been busy,' he said as his gaze wandered inadvertently over the swelling mound of his lady's bosom. Hastily he re-collected himself. 'Yes. Very busy. Government affairs, you know.'

'I hope you have been able to spare a few moments to enjoy Teresa's company,' said Lord Carrisford suavely. 'I am pleased to see that she does not look neglected.'

Teresa, understanding her name if nothing else, smiled brightly at Lord Carrisford, then moved closer to Sir Geoffrey Hume. Her magnificent black eyes were languorous, and the voluptuousness of her body perfectly evident through the tightly-stretched satin of her gown. Sir Geoffrey smirked contentedly.

'Marvellous woman, Carrisford.' He chucked her obligingly under the chin, and she purred in complacent response. 'Never needs entertaining, just smiles and eats. Don't know why she doesn't get fat.' He glanced down ruefully at his own well-corseted roundness. 'Comes to the play as willingly as if she understood every word of it, and then I don't have to listen to her chatter on the way home. So long as she doesn't learn to speak English, I should think we shall very likely suit for ever.'

'You are unlikely to have any problems in that direction,' said Lord Carrisford. 'I spent two months in her company and I am perfectly convinced that Teresa nourishes no secret desire to learn *anything*. Provided your servants keep her well supplied with sugar plums you need fear no sudden bursts of intellectual curiosity.'

Caroline wondered if she imagined the faint note of scorn that crept into Lord Carrisford's voice. Certainly, Sir Geoffrey

Hume was content merely to beam delightedly at the satisfactory nature of his friend's information.

'Well, well,' he said again contentedly, 'I can only be thankful you decided to bring her back from Portugal. But enough about Teresa and my affairs.' He turned courteously to Caroline. 'We must not neglect your own lovely lady.' He bowed deeply over Caroline's hand, reluctantly extended towards Sir Geoffrey in response to a hidden nudge from Lord Carrisford. 'And looking more stunningly beautiful than I have ever seen you, my dear. Those jewels are just the job. No more than you deserve, I'm sure.'

'I feel that I have worked hard for every stone,' said Caroline, smiling brightly as if she had no idea of any unflattering interpretation that might be put upon her words.

Lord Carrisford stiffened at the words, but such subtlety was quite lost on Sir Geoffrey who merely bowed again and remarked to Lord Carrisford, 'I can see that you two are ideally suited. Fortunate night's work for both of us when we agreed to make the exchange. You must bring Caroline round for a little supper with us one evening. It's always pleasant to have a little relaxing company over a meal.'

Caroline seethed silently. Lord Carrisford's offer was even more insulting than she had originally thought. It was intolerable to learn that she had been bargained away in exchange for *Teresa*. Lord Carrisford merely inclined his head in civil acknowledgment of Sir Geoffrey's remarks. 'We shall look forward to joining you, sir, although my own time is rather fully occupied just at present. Like you yourself, my work for the government is making heavy inroads into my time.'

Sir Geoffrey had the grace to look a trifle self-conscious. 'Yes. Well, I can't claim that dancing attendance on Prinny is quite the same thing as your work for Lord Liverpool. He after all, is responsible for running this war, while Prinny has nothing to do except design uniforms for his officers.'

'I wish to God that Liverpool were as efficient at running the war as His Royal Highness is at designing uniforms,' said Lord Carrisford with sudden violence. Sir Geoffrey looked at him with immediate interest, but the announcement of another group of visitors put paid to further confidences. Caroline, her roaming gaze having discovered the presence of her stepbrother in the crush of the stalls, was fully occupied in warding off the gushing compliments of Lord Carrisford's acquaintance, while she prayed desperately that the movements in their box would not attract Philippe's eye.

She now realised that her worst nightmares concerning this evening's performance fell far short of the actual horrors. Lord Carrisford's friends treated her with a casual familiarity she found almost literally nauseous. Their eyes stripped away the protection of her silk gown, their hands lingered lasciviously upon her gloved hands. She was thankful that the presence in the theatre of so many respectable matrons made more openly licentious behaviour impossible. Before the interval was at an end, her eyes flashed a look of desperate appeal to Lord Carrisford. To her relief he managed to clear the box within a matter of seconds, leaving her feeling faint and slightly sick, but blessedly alone. He made no reference to their succession of visitors, but simply handed her a glass of cool water.

'Here,' he said quietly. 'You may care to take a few sips.'

He waited until some of her pallor had receded, then remarked casually, 'Is this the first time you have seen Mrs Siddons? She is an impressive sight, is she not? Although ridiculously miscast as a seventeen-year-old virgin.'

Caroline would not have noticed had Mrs Siddons been cast in the rôle of a newly-born baby, but she drew on her memories of previous performances by the actress and tried to make some intelligent response. She realised that Lord Carrisford wished to put her once more at her ease, and she was grateful to him for his instinctive understanding. Their calm conversation helped to restore her sense of dignity, and by the time the curtain rose upon the second part of the play, she was more in command of her emotions. She still had no interest in the outcome of the plot, but at least she was aware of the words mouthed by the actors and actresses pacing the stage.

The falling of the curtain to mark the second interval occurred all too soon. Caroline glanced down into the brightly-lighted pit, her eyes seeking a further sight of her brother. He was nowhere to be found, and she was unable to make up her mind whether such an absence boded good or ill. In one sense, however embarrassing an encounter with him would prove, it would be better for all the wheels to be set in motion so that this masquerade could speed to its conclusion. Before she could make up her mind what she wanted to happen next, her eye caught a flurry of movements in the box opposite, and she was just in time to observe the Dowager Baroness Carrisford leave the box, followed in stately progression by a meek-looking female, dressed even more shabbily than the Dowager, and a hatchet-faced maid. For a moment, Caroline's gloomy mood was lightened as she speculated on which unfortunate people were about to receive the dubious privilege of a visit from the Dowager. With his uncanny ability to read her thoughts Lord Carrisford leaned towards her and said softly, 'Aren't you glad that procession isn't heading in our direction?'

He surprised her into a short ripple of laughter, which was interrupted by a loud knock on the door of their box. Instinctively her hand tightened into a convulsive grip upon Lord Carrisford's arm. Gently he prised her fingers from his coat, murmuring, 'Really, Caroline, think of my tailor!' although his eyes remained warm with laughter.

It was thus that the Dowager Baroness found them as she stalked into the box, with the footman squawking unhappily behind her. In her first moment of acute discomfort Caroline noticed that the meek companion and the dour-faced maid had both remained outside. Only the Dowager, it seemed, was utterly indifferent to convention.

'Well, Richard,' she said loudly. 'What have you got to say for yourself?'

'Nothing, ma'am,' said Lord Carrisford with perfect equanimity. 'As you very well know, you should not be here.'

The Dowager snorted. 'Not be here, indeed! It's all right for you to go trailing your fancy pieces all over town, but I am expected to sit on the opposite side of the theatre and ignore you. And, I might point out, you haven't bothered to come and see me for nearly a month. Time for your whores, but not for me.' Here she cast a withering glance at Caroline. 'What have you got her all decked out like a Christmas ornament for? The gal's got decent skin and hair, so why are you dangling baubles all over her?'

Lord Carrisford was finally beginning to look flustered. The Dowager's voice rivalled that of a sergeant-major conducting a dress parade, and although the general hubbub of noise drowned out most individual sounds, it was certain that anyone passing by their box would hear every word.

'I shall be happy to call upon you first thing tomorrow morning. Now will you please try and behave like any other self-respecting female and remove yourself from this box?'

The Dowager gave no indication that she had heard a word of her son's harassed suggestion. 'Why don't you get married?' she asked loudly. 'It's time you thought about producing some heirs to the Carrisford name. Do you good to get married. No point in wasting all your blunt on fancy women when you could marry somebody who'll bring money *into* the family.'

Caroline had no idea how she expected Lord Carrisford to respond to his mother. In her wildest imaginings, however, she had never expected him to crush her to his side and clasp her hand tenderly to his bosom. 'Ah, Caroline!' he murmured soulfully. 'I realise now that I should have had the courage to speak to my Mama a long time ago. She is right, as always. I should marry you and secure the Carrisford succession as soon as possible. Why should we be hobbled by outdated conventions? If my mother may defy all the rules of polite society, why may not I?'

Here he shot the Dowager a withering glance before turning back to Caroline. 'My love, let us be married as quickly as we may be. Only say that you will be mine, and I shall ask my mother for her blessing on the match!'

Fortunately for Caroline, who felt that her histrionic powers had already been tested to the limit, the Dowager chose this moment to give every evidence of falling into an immediate apoplexy. Lord Carrisford was forced to rush to his mother's side and urge upon her the revivifying effects of a glass of cordial. She refused such refreshment with an air that suggested she had been offered a deep draft of poison, and swept from the door without a further glance in Caroline's direction. Lord Carrisford watched her retreat with a rueful expression.

'You are a wretched girl,' he said to Caroline, although he could not disguise the laughter that shook beneath his voice. 'I have never known anybody else who was so easily able to provoke me into saying and doing what I had no intention of saying or doing. Unfortunately, by tomorrow my mother will realise that it was all a hum, and then she will come storming round to Carrisford House making life miserable for both of us. Still, I must say that I have rarely known the redoubtable Dowager to be so quickly routed. We have been spared her presence for the rest of the evening at least.'

Caroline was shocked by the coldness of his voice. 'She is your mother, my lord. Surely she has only your best interests at heart?'

'My mother's only interest is in imposing her will irrevocably upon all those unfortunate enough to find themselves under her jurisdiction. It is a constant irritation to her that I am dependent upon her neither for income nor for anything else. Conversation with my mother consists of my mother making statements and then totally ignoring any response which may be given to her by anybody.'

'Perhaps she is deaf,' said Caroline. 'That would explain why she speaks so loudly.'

'Nonsense,' said Lord Carrisford shortly. 'She is merely stubborn.' He fell silent for a few minutes, then said uneasily, 'Even if she is deaf, that is no justification for constantly interfering in our lives. Besides, why has nobody else in the family thought of such an explanation?'

'Possibly because you are all so frightened of her that you have forgotten to think of her simply as another human being,' said Caroline.

'Frightened by my mother?' Lord Carrisford's expression told of his outrage at the thought. After a short silence he grinned a little sheepishly. 'Well, perhaps I was just a *little* in awe of her before I attained my majority. Not now, of course.'

'Of course not,' said Caroline equably. 'And anyway, she can't be completely deaf, because she heard what you said about marrying me.'

'And nearly got carried away with the apoplexy right on the spot.' Lord Carrisford could hardly contain a fresh burst of laughter. 'Oh, Caroline! It would almost be worth marrying you, just to see her face.'

'Surely such a sacrifice would be too great, even in the interests of defying your mother,' said Caroline sweetly.

Lord Carrisford stood very still. 'I am not sure that it would be a sacrifice at all,' he said quietly. 'Caroline, I wish . . . I wish . . .'

The nature of Lord Carrisford's wishes

remained for the time being unexpressed, since the footman chose that moment to enter the box once again. Relieved to usher in two visitors who stood upon all the proper ceremonies, he announced the arrivals in ringing tones. 'Monsewer, the Count de la Rivière and Monsewer Patin,' he said, before retiring to his post outside the door.

'Philippe!' Caroline turned pale, but she smiled a warm welcome, thrusting herself in front of Lord Carrisford in an instinctive wish to separate the two men from each other. 'We are so pleased to have you back in town!'

'We?' asked Philippe sarcastically. He caught himself up and dipped his head in the briefest and most formal of bows to Lord Carrisford. At the same time he seemed to recollect the presence of his companion. 'May I present M. Patin to you both?' he asked curtly. 'Patin, this is my . . .' He hesitated, then spoke again, even more curtly than before. 'This is Miss Adams, and her escort this evening is Lord Carrisford.'

M. Patin, a short man of medium colouring and mild aspect, was conspicuous only in the very neutrality of his clothing and manner. He acknowledged the introduction with conventional courtesy, smiling politely as he touched his hand to the tips of Caroline's fingers. 'It is a pleasure to meet such a beautiful ornament of London's society,' he said in heavily accented but grammatically flawless English. His eyes rested fleetingly on the sparkle of gems clustered around Caroline's arms and neck. 'An ornament indeed,' he murmured appreciatively. 'And it is certainly a pleasure to meet such a distinguished member of the British government,' he said, bowing towards Lord Carrisford.

'You exaggerate my meagre contributions,' said Lord Carrisford. 'I cannot imagine how my trivial activities could come to your attention?' He allowed his voice to rise into a slight question, and Philippe broke into the conversation with feverish haste.

'M. Patin was once the *intendant* upon our family estates,' he said. '*Intendant*, that means in English a bailiff. M. Patin has just now managed to escape from France.'

'How interesting,' said Lord Carrisford. 'He no doubt has many harrowing tales to tell of oppression and injustice under the Emperor's iron rule?'

'No,' said M. Patin blandly. 'The Emperor has no time to involve himself in the affairs of quite ordinary people such as myself.'

His answer seemed to surprise Lord Carrisford, but Caroline, whose nerves were frayed almost to breaking-point, could tolerate such cat-and-mouse tactics no longer.

'Where have you been, Philippe? I so much wanted to speak with you last week.'

He did not answer her question directly. 'I, too, would like to speak to you alone. Come outside and take a walk with me.'

Lord Carrisford, who had appeared absorbed in conversation with M. Patin, intervened at once. 'I do not think that is altogether a good idea, Monsieur le Comte.' To Caroline's ears, his voice gave mocking emphasis to Philippe's title. He looked apologetically at M. Patin and murmured insincerely, 'Forgive me for mentioning such matters in front of one who is hardly a member of the family, but Miss Adams is now under my protection, and I cannot permit her to wander the corridors with young gentlemen at will.'

Philippe threw Lord Carrisford a glance of mingled loathing and embarrassment. 'I am her brother, my lord.' The words seemed to stick in his throat.

'Stepbrother,' corrected Lord Carrisford

gently. 'And that fact is known to so few people.' Once more his glance fell with apparent casualness upon M. Patin. 'Only think how foolish I shall feel if I am left sitting alone while Caroline strolls about the corridors.'

Caroline held her breath, waiting for Philippe to respond to Lord Carrisford's blatant provocation. Philippe did indeed take several quick steps forward as if to strike a blow at Lord Carrisford's serenely smiling features, then he visibly restrained himself. His breathing was swift and shallow, evidence of the turmoil churning within him.

'Then I ask your permission to visit Caroline in Carrisford House, my lord. There is . . . family business . . . which I must discuss. I have private messages to deliver from my mother, the Comtesse.'

'But Miss Adams and I have no secrets, my dear boy. All between us is an open book.'

Caroline gave a small cry, snatching up her cloak and pulling it round her shoulders. 'I will walk with you, Philippe. I find the atmosphere in here intolerably oppressive. Perhaps it will be better outside.' She looked defiantly at Lord Carrisford as she spoke, but his eyes were hooded and she could not read his expression.

Her brother did not give Lord Carrisford an opportunity to prevent Caroline's defiance. Without even pretending to wait for his lordship's approval, he placed his arm around Caroline's waist and hustled her from the box. He seemed as anxious to escape from M. Patin as she was to avoid Lord Carrisford. Once they were outside, he shot a quick look up and down the deserted corridor, then grasped Caroline's hands in a gesture of despair. 'Oh God, Caroline!' he groaned. 'Why did you do it? Surely jewels, even the famous ones you are now wearing, could not persuade you to take such a disastrous step? Why did you not resist my mother's wretched advice?'

She winced at the distraught tone of his voice. It was difficult to think of anything to say, particularly since she expected to see Lord Carrisford descending upon them at any moment.

Anxiously she drew Philippe further away from the Carrisford box. 'How much has the Comtesse told you?' she asked. 'Surely you realise that she insisted upon my joining Lord Carrisford?'

Philippe's voice sank to an agitated murmur. 'Oh God! This is the devil of a mess!'

'I am already aware of that,' said Caroline tartly. 'But I don't suppose you have any brilliant suggestions as to how we are to get out of it?' She was horrified that she could not prevent a sharp tone of sarcasm from entering her voice and tried to soften her remarks. It was unjust to keep all news of her affairs from Philippe and then to blame him if she did not like the consequences. 'What has been going on, Philippe? Why did the Comtesse insist that I Should leave the house, and who is this M. Patin?' A burning rush of colour stained her cheeks, then faded away, leaving her even paler than before. 'Why are you now behaving so strangely towards Lord Carrisford? Does it not bother you that I am . . . that I seem . . .'

Philippe interrupted her hastily, as if the details of her liaison with Lord Carrisford were too painful to be spoken of. 'Don't!' he commanded curtly. 'Later, I shall be in a position to give Lord Carrisford the lesson he deserves. For now . . .' He paused uncertainly. 'For now, it is not possible. There is so much to tell you, Caroline. I hoped to keep you outside the tangle of our affairs until we had come to some arrangement with the French government. But now it is impossible. *Maman* was so worried about you, and meant only for the best in sending you from the house. It is a cruel blow of fate that Lord Carrisford should have been the man chosen to protect you. Just a week later and I would have known he was the one man you most needed to avoid!' He spoke rapidly, almost incoherently, his eyes constantly searching the corridor for the sight of M. Patin or Lord Carrisford. It was hard to recognise the carefree youth of Caroline's recollections in this wild-eyed and entirely serious man.

'Philippe . . .' Caroline hesitated on the brink of a confession, amazed at how reluctant she felt to break faith with Lord Carrisford by revealing the plot they had concocted. She thrust away the feeling of betrayal. How could her loyalties lie elsewhere than with the stepbrother she had cherished and protected for so long?

'Philippe,' she started again, but the noise of the door opening from Lord Carrisford's box rose over the general hum of distant conversation. Anxiously Philippe put his arm around Caroline's waist and drew her further away from the listening ears of the solitary footman.

'We cannot speak here,' he said. 'I must talk to you where we can be alone. Can you leave his house? Come to my lodgings to-morrow morning.'

'It would be better if we could meet at the Comtesse's house. There can be no objection to my visiting your mother.'

'No, no. It must be my lodgings. *Maman* is *distraite*, and Patin watches her all the time. Besides, she thinks only of events in France.'

'I shall try to come,' whispered Caroline. 'If I cannot leave the house unobserved I shall contrive to send you word.'

She felt her brother stiffen as she spoke, and she whirled round with a guilty exclamation. She knew, even before she looked into his cold grey eyes, exactly who was standing behind her.

Lord Carrisford bent his head in brief acknowledgement of Philippe's presence. 'Shall we go, Caroline, my love?' His words suggested the casual intimacy of old friends, although she at least was fully aware of the rage that burned beneath the innocuous words. 'I believe that this play has lost something of its savour for both of us. Mrs Siddons cannot be on form tonight.'

'Where is M. Patin?' asked Caroline stupidly. She felt dazed by the events of the evening, and distracted by the need to speak with her brother alone.

'M. Patin has gone to join the Comtesse,' said Lord Carrisford smoothly. 'He seems to share our opinion of tonight's performance and has decided not to wait for the final acts.' He nodded briefly to the silent Philippe. 'M. Patin entrusted me with a message for you, sir. He will await you at your mother's house.' He saw that Caroline still lingered uncertainly at her brother's side, and he took her hand firmly and placed it with seeming solicitude upon his arm.

'Come, my dear. Your adieux to M. le Comte have, I think, been sufficiently prolonged.'

She hoped for one last chance to arrange the details of the meeting with her brother. 'My reticule!' she exclaimed. 'It has been left by my chair.'

'No,' said Lord Carrisford smoothly. 'I was fortunate enough to observe that you had left it behind and retrieved it before I left the box. The footman is holding it for you.'

There was nothing to do but to smile as well as she was able towards Philippe. He bowed low over her extended hands, raising them to his lips and dropping a kiss on the tips of her fingers. But when he leant towards her to kiss her cheek, she pulled away, fearful lest he commit the indiscretion of trying to whisper some secret instruction to her while Lord Carrisford looked on. She knew he did not understand the gesture of withdrawal, and she was forced to walk away from him leaving him alone in the corridor. His shoulders drooped with a weary resignation, and her heart contracted with sympathy. What had happened to the smiling young man who had laughed and flirted with her on her birthday? And was Philippe truly changed, or had Lord Carrisford merely opened her eyes to the realities of his personality?

She carried the uncomfortable thought with her to the carriage and allowed the memory of her brother's forlorn figure to haunt her during the short journey home.

Chapter Ten

THE realisation of danger invaded Caroline's dreams, stiffening her limbs and filling her ears with the pounding thud of her heart-beats. She felt the hand close over her mouth even before she was properly awake, and a rush of terror jerked her upright in the curtained bed. She could not scream, but she could struggle, and she kicked her legs fiercely against the restraining weight of the bedcovers.

'For God's sake do not make such a noise,' whispered Philippe's familiar voice. Her scuffling ceased abruptly, and he withdrew his hand from her mouth. 'Is Carrisford likely to come into your room, or are we safe for a short while?' He made no effort to disguise his nervousness. Dust streaks marred the black velvet of his jacket, and his face was unusually pallid.

'Philippe! You should not be in my bedroom . . .' She stopped herself in the middle of the foolish reprimand. She had spent the entire day trying unsuccessfully to escape from Lord Carrisford's eagle-eyed observation, and she realised, now that she was properly awake, that this clandestine meeting was the only practical way of achieving a private conversation with her brother. Thinking of the painful hours passed under Lord Carrisford's cold scrutiny, she still could not admit how much she had been hurt by his all-too-evident lack of trust. Nor would she admit that the passage of every moment in Lord Carrisford's company had made her more reluctant to justify his suspicions by warning Philippe of the traps that had been set for him.

'Caroline!' Philippe's insistent whisper brought her back to the realities of the present. 'Will Lord Carrisford come in again tonight?'

'No,' she said, not bothering to explain that Lord Carrisford never came into her bedroom after dark. 'He will not be coming. How did *you* get in?'

'Through a window in the kitchen,' he said, dismissing the question impatiently. 'What has Carrisford told you about the other Comte de la Rivière?' His nervous gaze flickered from the door to the window and back again. 'Quickly, Caroline! You must tell me everything.'

'Carrisford met the other count, Count André, in Portugal. André claims to be your father's eldest son, who has only now discovered the facts of his inheritance. He wishes to support the Royalist cause and he has valuable information about Bonaparte's campaign plans that he is willing to sell to the Allies. Lord Carrisford is not sure whether or not to trust him.' She could not bring herself to add the final, damning piece of information: that Carrisford believed Philippe himself to be a Bonapartist agent.

'You *must* convince Carrisford that Count André is the legitimate heir,' said Philippe. 'Caroline, I did not want you to be involved in these matters which are the misfortunes of our family, not yours. But it is a matter of life and death for Lord Carrisford to be convinced that André is the true heir to the Rivière estates. You must try to persuade Carrisford that André is indeed a Royalist agent.'

'Are you mad?' whispered Caroline. 'Are you telling me that he is, in fact, your older brother?'

Philippe's lips twisted into a cynical smile. 'He is, at any rate, my father's son, and a couple of years older than I myself.'

'Oh!' Caroline assimilated the information. 'But why should you wish to acknowledge your father's . . . your father's . . .'

'Why do I wish to acknowledge my father's bastard child as the heir to my estates? Is that what you wish to ask me, Caroline?'

'Yes.'

'Oh God! I wish I knew what would be for the best. Whether to tell you or to keep you in ignorance of the whole. Your honest face, *chérie*, is not well adapted for the keeping of secrets.'

'If you have betrayed your country, Philippe, I think it would be better if you did not tell me. I could not undertake to keep such information silent.'

'My country? And what land is that, may I ask? England, where Carrisford and his friends are pleased to look down upon me as a professional gambler? The France of M. Bonaparte, which denies to me the inheritance which is justifiably mine? Do not speak to me of countries, Caroline. It is sufficient if I am able to protect my family and to spare my mother further suffering.'

Caroline allowed herself to feel encouraged. Such a speech did not seem the likely outburst of one of England's foremost Bonapartist agents. 'And does your mother agree with this insanity of yours? She is encouraging you to acknowledge a bastard as the heir to your father's lands?' She turned to him with sudden accusation in her voice. 'M. Patin! *He* has something to do with this, does he not?'

'Forget about M. Patin, Caroline. It is chiefly for my mother's sake that I am embroiled in this mess. It is for her, Caroline, and I beg you to help me although I have no right to ask it of you.'

'But you must tell me what this is all about, Philippe. Surely you did not take so many risks just to come here and tell me that you can tell me nothing?' She tried to reassure him by recapturing some of their old childhood affection. 'Philly, my love, you know how often I have been able to aid you out of some scrape when you had decided that retribution was inevitable. May I not be allowed to help you now?'

He answered slowly, without looking at her, as though he could scarcely trust himself to speak. 'An agent for the French government has told my mother that . . . that somebody important to her is being held as a prisoner in one of the gaols in Paris.'

'Philippe! Who . . .' Her voice died away into a horrified whisper as they both heard a faint creak in the floorboards. Philippe cringed back into the shadowed depths of the bed curtains. They waited in tense si-

169

lence, their fingers locked in a rigid clasp of mutual reassurance, but no further sound disturbed the stillness of the night. But Philippe's fragile confidence was shattered. He leaned over and spoke close against Caroline's ear as if he suspected the very bed-posts of listening to their conversation. 'I dare not confide in you any further. I have already said too much. Only strive your utmost to convince Carrisford that André is my brother and that his word may be trusted. Carrisford must be *made* to believe that André's information is correct. I beg of you, Caroline, do your best! If not for my sake, then for the sake of my mother.'

'I could call upon the Comtesse tomorrow,' suggested Caroline. 'Lord Carrisford surely cannot refuse to allow such a visit. We could meet there early in the morning.'

'No, no! Patin will be there! I had the devil's own job to lose him tonight. Promise me you won't go?' His whisper rose hysterically, and he seized both her hands in an impassioned plea.

The blaze of candlelight disturbed them almost before they heard the door of the dressing-room bang open.

'You!' whispered Caroline.

'Carrisford!' exclaimed Philippe.

'Forgive me for intruding upon such a touching scene,' said Lord Carrisford. 'But I feel this is hardly the time to be exchanging sibling secrets.'

'I had messages to deliver to Caroline from my mother. Madame la Comtesse is not well.' Philippe struggled to stand upon his dignity, but succeeded only in sounding defiant and more than a little frightened.

'The Comtesse de la Rivière is welcome to call upon me at any time. She is also at liberty to send one of her servants with messages if she is too unwell to remove from her house.' He smiled at Caroline, a glittering smile that lacked any pretence of warmth or affection. 'You, I believe, have already been warned of my feelings concerning the bestowal of your favours. Your exclusive services have already been bought, by me.'

She hated him for the false impression he was creating in Philippe's mind. 'But those services are not yet paid for, my lord,' she spat out, though her hands shook beneath the covers. 'You may recall that I returned the money that was supposed to buy my favours.'

He laughed harshly. 'There is always the little collection of trinkets that you wore last night. I imagine *your* experienced eyes were not deceived for a moment by my story about fakes. Perhaps you sought your step-brother's assistance in arranging for a sale. Is that why he has broken into my house?'

She gasped at the insult, unable to reply immediately because of the lump of misery choking her throat. Although Lord Carrisford's voice remained cold, she knew him too well to be deceived, and she saw that he hovered on the brink of almost uncontrollable rage. 'Go now,' she said to Philippe, laying her hand reassuringly on his arm.

'Perhaps it is necessary for me to stay.' Philippe moved away from the bed and faced firmly up to Lord Carrisford. His slender body presented a poignant contrast to the commanding strength of Lord Carrisford's tall figure.

'Despite everything, I shall kill you if Caroline is harmed,' he said flatly.

Lord Carrisford turned away with a sharp exclamation of annoyance. 'Your sister stands in no danger from me. You had better go. The front door is unbarred now. Pray avail yourself of its convenient service. It will save you the cost of a further bribe to the kitchen-maid.'

Philippe did not deign to reply to this final piece of mockery. '*Au revoir*, Caroline.' He kissed her shaking fingers, but did not speak again to Lord Carrisford. The door shut quietly behind him.

Lord Carrisford allowed the silence to stretch out, straining Caroline's already taut nerves to breaking-point. Her whole body trembled now that Philippe was actually gone, and guilt overwhelmed her. It seemed that she was destined to betray either her brother or the man she loved. As the shocking implications of that last thought became plain to her, she felt the tears shiver on the brink of her lashes. She *could* not allow herself to fall in love with Lord Carrisford now. Defiantly she dashed the tears away then raised her eyes to Lord Carrisford's face. He returned her gaze with a shaft of such burning fury that she instinctively shrank back against the pillows.

'You might be good enough—now that we are at last alone—to tell me what the *hell* you think you are about.' Although his voice remained glacially cold, his eyes betrayed the extent of his anger. There was no point in pretending that she did not understand his question.

'I did not invite Philippe to my room, my

lord. He came on his own initiative because you seemed determined to prevent any private conversation between the two of us.'

'Naturally I prevented you speaking to Philippe. I must remind you that I suspect him of being an agent in the pay of Napoleon's imperial armies. What did you tell him during your private conversation? Or were you too preoccupied in offering *sisterly* comforts to spare time for the trivial exchange of information?'

'Your innuendoes are despicable, my lord. Philippe, naturally enough, sought an explanation for your strange interest in the activities of Count André. I told Philippe that you were interested in discovering whether or not Count André's claim to the Rivière estate is valid.'

Lord Carrisford's eyes seemed to burn inside her mind, causing her to squirm uneasily at the memory of all she was leaving unsaid. 'If you told Philippe so little, what did he see fit to tell you? I suppose that is the question which should interest us most.'

She wished she could dissemble and pretend that Philippe had revealed nothing at all, that he had given her no instructions regarding her behaviour towards Lord Carrisford. She looked up at him, the lies already forming on her lips. It was a mistake to have looked away from the counterpane, for the cool grey eyes pierced her defences and she shivered visibly, although not from fear. The lies died away unspoken. 'Philippe wants you to believe that Count André is the true heir to the Rivière estates,' she said dully.

'And is he? Philippe acknowledges that this man is his older brother and thus has a better claim to the title than Philippe himself?'

She knew better than to risk meeting his gaze this time. 'I don't know, my lord. Philippe did not discuss his own rights with me.'

'No?' Lord Carrisford did not bother to disguise his scepticism. 'Philippe has such ample evidence of your devotion to his cause. I find it hard to believe that he did not confide in you upon so important a matter.'

The jeering contempt of his questions pierced the confusion of her emotions. Suddenly she no longer wished to cower under the bedclothes, cringing from his attack. She welcomed the rage that flowed through her limbs, liberating her from the debilitating lethargy that confined her. She thrust back the covers and sprang from the bed, indifferent to the appearance she presented in her thin bed-gown. She experienced a moment of triumph as she heard the swift, harsh intake of his breath and knew that he found her desirable.

'No, my lord,' she hissed. 'Philippe did not choose to confide in me. He thinks I am your mistress.' She laughed gratingly. 'No doubt he suspects the purity of my loyalties as much as he fears for the purity of my morals. You have set up your little subterfuges too well, my lord. Philippe is unlikely to confide his innermost secrets to another man's doxy!'

'Be silent!' He seized her shoulders in a moment of violent anger. She stared up at him recklessly, protected by her armour of rage. With admirable detachment, she observed the slight tan that still tinged his complexion and the recent scar, memento of an unknown battle, which stood out as a white triangle on the high plane of his cheek-bone. She could see the exact moment when the fury lurking in the depths of his eyes changed to passion of a different kind and, at the same moment, she discovered a fatal chink in her armour. She struggled desperately to get out of his arms, but her lips quivered into an instant response as soon as she felt the demanding pressure of his mouth against her own. The silver buttons of his evening-coat pressed into her breast, and she shuddered with the strength of her feelings.

As suddenly as he had possessed her, he pushed her out of his arms, derision twisting his lips into a sneer. 'Do not bother to exert your wiles on me, Madam. You will catch cold at that even if you are damn near desirable enough to cause a king to whistle his kingdom to the winds.'

She wanted to be folded back within the warmth of his arms, and to whisper that she was his for the asking. But some tiny remnant of common sense enabled her to walk back to the bed, keeping her gaze averted so that he would not see the naked longing in her eyes. 'Am I to be permitted any sleep tonight, my lord? Or do my duties include listening to ridiculous accusations at three in the morning?'

He was standing by the fireplace when she finally turned round. His face hidden by the shadows in that corner of the room. 'You will present yourself in my library at ten o'clock tomorrow morning,' he said. 'I have one more task for you to perform, and then I shall be at liberty to make the arrangements for your removal from my house. Believe me, Madam, you cannot look forward to that moment more fervently than I do myself.'

'I will perform no more tasks for you, my lord. I have decided that I do not like the rôle of government agent.'

'I will see you in the library at ten o'clock tomorrow morning, Miss Adams. If you are not there, a warrant for your brother's arrest will be issued before noon.' He paused at the dressing-room door and bowed slightly. 'Until tomorrow morning, Miss Adams. I am looking forward to our meeting.'

Chapter Eleven

CAROLINE was awake long before Bessie brought in the tray of hot chocolate. She watched the servant place the silver pot on a small table near the hearth and draw back the heavy curtains at the window. The ritual completed, Bessie came and stood by Caroline's bed, her hands clasped meekly across her apron, her eyes turned carefully away from the occupant of the bed.

'I have brought your morning chocolate,

Miss.' The perfect politeness and absolute coldness of her voice combined to make the simple sentence a jewel in the art of deliberate insult.

'Thank you, Bessie.' Caroline responded calmly, as she did every morning, although today she would have liked to spit out a few insults of her own. She nodded her dismissal to the maid.

'That will be all, Bessie,' she said politely, just as she had done every morning for the past two weeks.

Bessie bobbed a slight curtsy, but she did not immediately hurry from the room.

'You look pale, Miss, pardon the liberty in speaking so free. Would you like me to close the curtains so you can get some more sleep?' For once there seemed to be no sarcasm underlining the polite enquiry.

Caroline fought against the cowardly desire to accept the escape route Bessie offered. She could retreat back under the covers and pretend she was sick. The thought was tempting, but only for a moment. There was really no point in postponing the confrontation with Lord Carrisford. If she stayed in bed today he would merely make his demands tomorrow.

'Thank you, Bessie, but I am not tired. Lord Carrisford is waiting to see me.'

'As you wish, Miss.' Bessie's voice indicated that she already regretted her brief excursion into normal human sympathy, and Caroline sighed. Her own conscience was troublesome enough without needing the constant reminders provided by Bessie's frowning presence.

'Perhaps you would send Mary and Margaret up with some hot water,' she said. 'I think I shall take a bath. I know you will see to it all as quickly as possible, since your master is waiting.'

'Very good, Miss.' No request could have been more calculated to offend the housekeeper, who was of the firm opinion that total immersion of the body, particularly with the frequency desired by Miss Adams, was a sign of wantonness unsurpassed in Bessie's previous experience. A naked body and hot, perfumed water could only be expected to lead to sin, and Bessie wished she had the authority to prevent the maids attending such a sybaritic performance. Alas, she had no such powers, and was forced merely to purse her lips and make sure that That Woman was fully aware of the enormity of her wickedness. Caroline, after one

180

look, had no difficulty in perceiving that she had already fallen from her foothold on the stairway to Bessie's approval. She watched the housekeeper's silent exit with regret. She was not used to being on such uncomfortable terms with the people who served her.

The memory of this early-morning scene did nothing to boost Caroline's confidence as she stood hesitantly outside Lord Carrisford's study door. Responding to some whim that she did not fully understand and preferred not to examine, she had dressed herself for the interview in a gown of sprigged yellow muslin that emphasised the blazing gold of her hair and the perfection of her smooth complexion. Her toilette had taken some time to effect, and the hands of her watch now pointed accusingly to seven minutes after the hour of ten o'clock. She knew that she should be knocking on Lord Carrisford's door, but instead she stood outside shuffling her feet and fiddling with the embroidered ends of her yellow satin sash. Finally, conscious of the fact that a young footman had been trying to avoid staring at her for the past several minutes, she raised her hand and tapped firmly on the panels of the door.

'Enter!' The command was snapped out in the curtest possible tone, and her chin lifted defiantly. She would not let him see that her knees already banged together in trepidation at what was to come. She walked into the room as gaily as though she had not a care in the world. A more poetic man than Lord Carrisford might have thought that Caroline, in her yellow dress, brought memories of sunlight and summer flowers into the dark solemnity of his book-room. Lord Carrisford merely looked at her in impenetrable silence, before saying brusquely, 'You are eight minutes late for our appointment.'

'I find it so hard to wake promptly after a disturbed night.' She smiled at him sweetly, opening her brown velvety eyes very wide. Some instinct told her that he found such flirtatious tactics as difficult to handle as she found his icy stares. When he did not immediately respond, she walked over to his bookshelves and idly plucked one of the volumes from its dusty niche. She flipped over several pages and gave a small, affected laugh.

'La, sir! I have found a job for Bessie at last. Other than scowling at me, of course. You may set her and the maids to dusting your bookshelves, for they certainly need it.'

In two strides he came round from his desk and stood beside her, snatching the book from her hands. 'Is nothing safe from your presence?' he said fiercely. 'You invade my house, upset my routine. Even my valet will scarcely speak to me because he has chosen to disapprove of my treatment of you. Now you must start organising my library! It is enough, Madam. It is time to call a halt to this farcical masquerade!'

She was astonished at the bitterness of his outburst, for her own actions scarcely justified such a violent reaction. She did not answer his string of accusations, but said simply, 'We are finally in agreement, my lord. It is certainly time to end this masquerade. Do I have your permission to rejoin my stepmother?'

She had never before seen so desolate an expression in Lord Carrisford's eyes. It was a moment or two before he spoke, and then he said in a level tone, drained of all his previous anger, 'I realise that our liaison has been a mistake. But I cannot permit you to return to the Comtesse's house. I have a certain duty towards my government which must be fulfilled.'

'God forbid that you should neglect your duty.' She did not try to conceal the resentment in her voice.

'Do you think that you are the only one to find yourself in a position that is distasteful to you?' His hand clenched tightly around the book. 'Enough!' he said. 'I have called you here for a purpose. I have already sent a message to your brother, purporting to be from you. In your name I have requested his presence here before noon, and I have informed him that he will be at liberty to hold a private conversation with you.'

Caroline's eyes shone with unexpected gratitude. 'That is very generous of you, my lord.'

'It is no such thing,' he said harshly, unable to tear his gaze from the sparkle of her eyes. 'I expect you to coax Philippe into telling you everything that he knows concerning Count André. Since I place no reliance whatsoever upon your willingness to repeat what Philippe has confided to you, I shall conceal myself and eavesdrop upon the conversation.'

She did not bother to consider how distasteful Lord Carrisford would find it to eavesdrop upon a private conversation. She only gave herself time to think that she was once more being forced into the intolerable position of betraying somebody who loved and trusted her.

'Is nothing too contemptible for you to undertake in your harassment of my family?' she asked scornfully, and took pleasure in seeing him pale slightly beneath his tan. 'And what threat do you hold over my head this time? If Philippe does not pour family confidences into your ears is he to be clapped in gaol? Or this time do you perhaps plan to threaten the Comtesse as well? You have stooped to everything else, why should you balk at incriminating an elderly lady who has already suffered the loss of everything she holds most dear.'

For a moment it seemed that Lord Carrisford would not answer her. He placed the book back on the shelf with meticulous care, and when he again turned to face Caroline his face was clean of emotion. 'There is a small sitting-room on the first floor,' he said quietly. 'It contains a large Chinese screen, an excellent example of the work of the Ming dynasty. I shall sit behind the screen. You will oblige me by keeping Philippe at the other end of the room. That should not be difficult, since the screen is in the corner furthest from the fireplace and it is chilly this morning.'

'You cannot expect me to do this!' said Caroline, although she knew very well that he did.

Lord Carrisford ignored the comment. 'Please make sure that Philippe explains why he is so interested in furthering Count André's claims. I should also like to know why M. Patin is suddenly able to escape from France and why he has chosen to do so. I cannot imagine that a woman of your capabilities will have any difficulty in eliciting such information.' He was careful to avoid looking at her while he spoke.

'So now I am to betray my brother's confidence in me,' she said. 'How am I to be rewarded? With thirty pieces of silver, or are you prepared to pay me off more handsomely than that?' She twisted her hands together in a gesture of dispair. 'Oh, I should have fled from my stepmother's house when I had the chance! I shall never forgive myself for being so craven as to enter Carrisford House. I could have found work *somewhere.*'

Her last words were scarcely more than an anguished murmur, certainly not intended to arouse Lord Carrisford's sympathy.

'Caroline . . .' He moved towards her with a gesture of supplication that she failed to observe through the mist of angry tears. 'All the evidence is against you, Caroline.' She paid no heed to the note of entreaty in his voice, but hunched her shoulders in defiant rejection. 'How can I allow my own feelings to sway me? Hundreds of lives will be saved if Wellington is given accurate information. Napoleon boasts of mounting a personal campaign in Spain, but the *guerrilleros* say that his armies in Spain are spread too thin even to defend the garrison towns. Which story is correct?' He seized her arm with renewed ferocity, as if unwilling to listen to further discussion, and half-dragged her from the library.

After the first few undignified steps, she did not try to stop him, for she retained sufficient charge of her wits to realise that physical resistance to a man of Lord Carrisford's strength was folly of the most useless kind. She did not see that Bessie stood in a corner of the hall, and it would not have occurred to Caroline to seek the servant's help even if she had. Bessie watched Caroline's reluctant progress with a blank expression but, just for a moment, her frowning gaze was fixed reprovingly on her master.

The small sitting-room which Lord Carrisford finally entered was unfamiliar to Caroline, but she wasted no time in admiring its Oriental furnishings and elegant satin-striped wallpaper. 'Please take your hands from my arm, my lord,' she said with icy formality. He complied at once, and as soon as she was free she moved to the point of the room furthest from his side. She kept her eyes deliberately averted from his face, not daring to risk contact with his burning gaze.

'I shall do as you wish, my lord,' she said as if there had been no interruption of their discussion. 'Not because you ask me to, nor even because you think you have the means to compel me. I shall do it because I do not believe that my stepbrother is a traitor to the country that has provided him with a home all these years. I will ask him the questions, my lord, so that I may have the pleasure of hearing you *beg* for my pardon, and for his.'

'We shall wait the outcome of the meeting,' said Lord Carrisford with seeming indifference. 'I am afraid that you must remain here with me until Philippe arrives. I cannot risk having you sneak any private conversation with him before he joins us.'

'As you wish, my lord. If you keep me prisoner here, even you will be satisfied that there has been no collusion.'

She did not look at him after saying this, but sat down in one of the chairs furthest from the painted screen. It seemed an eternity that she waited there, mute and resentful, but at last Lord Carrisford turned away from the window.

'Your brother is arriving now,' he said. 'I have just seen him get out of a hackney-carriage.' He did not wait for her to acknowledge his remark, but placed himself behind the screen. He was, Caroline realised regretfully, quite invisible. Not even a shadow hinted at the presence in the room of anybody other than herself. She waited, in numb resignation, for the sound of her brother's footsteps.

It was only a few minutes until he walked into the room. He followed closely behind Atkins, and greeted her with a warm embrace, barely waiting for the butler to leave the room before speaking excitedly.

'Caroline, this is marvellous! The dragon permits us to be alone. What miracles have you wrought to bring him under your thumb?'

She could not help stiffening at the words, and returned his embrace half-heartedly. Now, if ever, was the moment to warn him of Lord Carrisford's presence. She did not doubt that she could do it. They had shared so many childhood secrets, how easy it would be to make some slight gesture that would warn Philippe to beware. But she merely said quietly, 'We must not waste precious time, Philippe, and I beg you not to put me off with any more of your equivocations. Answer me honestly, if you please. What is so disastrous about my liaison with Lord Carrisford? And what is the great mystery surrounding Count André's sudden appearance in our lives?'

'Hush!' he begged her, and walked soundlessly to the door. He pulled it open with a jerk, and then pushed it shut again with a sigh of relief. 'I have learned these past few days not to trust the servants,' he said wryly. 'Ah, Caroline, I fear the only intrigue I am capable of conducting is one of the heart. Count André has missed his guess in expecting *me* to further the Bonapartist cause.'

She thought for a moment that her heart

would stop beating, and she felt the blood drain from her cheeks. 'I do not think I understand you, Philippe. Please tell me that I have not understood you aright?'

'Caroline, *chérie*, do not look at me so.' He gathered her rigid body into his arms, and stroked her hair lovingly. 'I should not burden you with our troubles,' he said softly. 'But I have relied upon you ever since I can remember, and I must confide in somebody or I fear I shall go mad. With my mother I must strive to be calm, with my friends I must laugh and joke. Only with you can I be myself.'

'Tell me about Count André,' said Caroline, standing stiffly within the circle of his arms.

'Last night I only had time to tell you that André is my father's son, born out of wedlock three years before I myself. In fact, André was conceived even before my father was married to my mother. When the child was born, he was boarded with the Patins, and every provision was made for his future. It was intended that he should be trained as a lawyer and funds were put in trust for him.' Philippe gave a small, bitter laugh. 'You will observe that my father was not the monster of inhumanity that his enemies pretend. I doubt if many Englishmen would have made better provision for a bastard child.'

'But André has some hold over you now, Philippe, does he not? Otherwise, how can it matter to you what this man does in France? If Napoleon's government recognises him as the heir to the Rivière estates, there is surely nothing you can do?' She placed her hand pleadingly upon his arm. 'You would not consider bargaining with the Emperor's band of traitors just for the sake of some land? Philippe, I know you would not!'

'I have no interest in bargaining for my lands, Caroline. I accept that they are lost to me and, if they were not, the various armies have marched back and forth across them so many times that I doubt if the vineyards now produce anything more than a luxurious crop of weeds. No. They have found a better hold over me than the promise of lands and titles. They have told us that my father is still alive and that—for a price—they will return him to us.'

'Your father!' Caroline sank into the chair. 'Oh, dear heaven! Why did the Comtesse not confide in me?' In her agitation, she forgot entirely about Lord Carrisford, still concealed behind the screen. She rose to her feet, wrapping a gossamer-fine shawl tightly round her shoulders. 'We must go to your mother,' she said. 'Oh, Philippe, how she must have been suffering! I must be at fault that she did not choose to confide in me. Why are you waiting, Philippe? Let us go to her at once!'

'Caroline, only think for a moment.' Gently he took her arm and pressed her back into the chair. 'You will achieve nothing useful by rushing to my mother's side. The Comtesse has known for more than a month that my father escaped the guillotine. According to our informant, he has been imprisoned ever since Robespierre first issued the warrant for his arrest. At first my mother would not believe the news. The message came at the hands of a disreputable French sailor, and she imagined that, having deserted his ship, he merely wished to make himself a few extra pennies. The sailor claimed to be a courier for the Bonapartists in this country, so of course *Maman* demanded proof. It came in the form of a letter from my father, which was delivered by one of the French *émigrés*. M. Patin has brought us a second, and longer message. My father has explained about the existence of his son, and he has told us that the French government plans to use André as part of their scheme to confuse British military agents working in the Peninsula. It seems that the intelligence the British army has been gathering from the Spanish *guerrilleros* has been too accurate, and Napoleon is striving to confuse the situation. He does not like the direction of Wellington's planning at all.'

'How can I have been so blind?' asked Caroline miserably. 'I saw that my stepmother was worried, but I assumed she was troubled over finances or some other trivial matter. Why did she not take me into her confidence, Philippe?'

'My mother has been worrying for months about the unsettled state of your future, Caroline, and this problem was the final straw. She could only think that if we were to be involved in dangerous tricks and stratagems in order to save my father's life, then you had to be securely established elsewhere. I knew what was in her mind, of course, but had no idea what method she was planning to adopt to get you settled.'

'If only the Comtesse had told me what was happening!' said Caroline. 'As if I would have left her at such a time!'

'That is precisely why she did not tell you

what was going on,' said Philippe. 'And that is why I, too, was kept in the dark until the last possible moment. Only after you had left the house did I discover the full truth about Count André. And it was only after I had been to Dover last week to collect M. Patin that I learned the name of the government official here in London whom the French most want to deceive. It is, of course, Lord Carrisford. He is the liaison between the civilian government and the army, and he is responsible for passing final judgement on the accuracy on André's information. You may imagine how I reacted to my mother's news that Lord Carrisford had been appointed as your *protector!*'

Philippe misunderstood the stricken look on Caroline's face. She had just remembered the presence of Lord Carrisford behind the screen and was cursing herself silently for having allowed Philippe to reveal so much. She raised her hand to stop her brother speaking, but he caught her fingers in his grasp and dropped a tiny, affectionate kiss upon the inside of her wrist.

'*Chérie,* now you understand why it is so important for us to convince Lord Carrisford that Count André is an ardent supporter of the Royalist cause, and that

André's reports will aid British military planning. The safety of my father has been made conditional upon the success of André's mission. If Carrisford acts upon the information he is being passed by Count André, then my father goes free. The French government will arrange for him to be placed in a smuggler's boat in Calais, and he may live out his final years in freedom, here with his family.'

Caroline started to speak, to warn him of Lord Carrisford's presence in the room, but he interrupted her curtly. 'Do not tell me that I am betraying your country, Caroline. Do not speak to me of treason. It is my father's life and my mother's happiness which lies within the palm of my hand. My mother and I have only to support the false claims of my half-brother. That is a small exchange for my father's freedom.'

'Philippe, do not say any more . . .' Now, at last, she was determined to warn him, even though she would have to bear the brunt of Lord Carrisford's anger. But there was no time for the confession which hovered on the brink of her lips, for Lord Carrisford pushed aside the screen and stepped out into Philippe's plain view.

'I, too, think that you have said enough,' he said quietly.

Philippe stared at Lord Carrisford for one long moment, then he thrust Caroline away from his side with a gesture of utter contempt.

'So! Suspecting the servants was an insufficient precaution,' he said. 'Take your whore, my lord, she has served you well.' His scornful eyes raked the deathly pallor of Caroline's complexion. 'Pray tell me dear *sister*, what was he able to give you that meant so much more than all our years of love and family affection? Surely a betrayal of such magnitude is worth a considerable sum? I hope you bargained well.'

Caroline tried to speak, but her voice broke on the very first word. Philippe dropped his gaze to the floor, but the memory of his hard, hate-filled eyes brought tears to the edge of her lashes. 'It is not quite as it s-seems, Philippe.'

She wanted to touch him, but Lord Carrisford took her outstretched arm and held her by his side. A tremble started in her legs and spread through her whole body. She wondered inconsequentially if Lord Carrisford could feel how violently she was shaking. 'I will explain everything to you later,

Philippe,' she said, and walked blindly towards the door.

'Caroline!' It was Lord Carrisford who called out to her, but she was past the point of heeding anyone's voice. She pushed through the door and ran along the corridor, indifferent to the direction of her flight. She stopped only when a baize-covered door barred her passage, and then she leaned her burning cheeks against its scratchy panels, gasping for air as though she had recently escaped from drowning.

'Are you all right, Miss?'

Never had she thought that Bessie's voice would sound so welcome. She struggled with a ludicrous impulse to rest her head on Bessie's shoulder and burst into tears.

'Miss?' Bessie placed a tentative hand on Caroline's arm. 'Shall I take you to your room, Miss?'

There was no point in trying to pretend that everything was all right. One look at her face would reveal the truth. 'Bessie, I need help. I must leave Carrisford House at once.'

'Yes, Miss. I Think that would be for the best.'

Caroline knew that the housekeeper had misunderstood the situation, but she was too distraught to spend time correcting Bessie's mistaken impressions. 'Will you help me pack a few things, Bessie? And perhaps I could leave through the servants' entrance. It would save questions later on.'

'Yes, Miss.' Bessie opened the door of Caroline's room and led her unresistingly to the armchair by the side of the fire. 'I'll bring you some tea, Miss, and then you shall tell me just what I am to pack. It's never too late to make a fresh start, Miss, if you don't mind me saying so.'

It was impossible even to begin explaining the truth, and Caroline was content simply to feel grateful for the calm sympathy of the housekeeper's manner. 'Thank you, Bessie,' she said. 'I would appreciate some tea.'

'Men are blind most often,' said Bessie irrelevantly. 'But I had always hoped Lord Carrisford was something special.'

'I think he is,' said Caroline sadly.

'Never mind, Miss. I'll bring you the tea.'

Chapter Twelve

THE interior of the hackney-carriage smelled musty, and Caroline moved her feet distastefully away from a heap of damp straw. She removed a clean white handkerchief from her reticule and wiped determinedly at the obstinate trickles of moisture escaping down her cheeks.

Her tears were scarcely dry when the hackney swayed to a halt and the jarvey opened the door with a friendly smile.

'This 'ere is number ten, Mount Street, ma'am.'

'Thank you.' She paused in the act of paying him off. 'Would you please wait for me? I'm not sure if the lady I have come to visit will be there.'

The jarvey nodded politely. 'I'll keep your bag in the carriage, ma'am. Save you carrying something heavy if your party doesn't 'appen to be 'ome.'

She smiled at him gratefully and walked slowly up the stairs, no longer trying to pretend that her situation was an enviable one. She had virtually no money, no prospect of employment and nowhere to go if the Comtesse refused her shelter.

It was reassuring, therefore, to be greeted by Jenk's familiar smile. He conducted her into the entrance lobby, chattering warmly. 'Nice to see you, Miss. I knew you wouldn't be long in paying us a call once you knew the Comtesse was feeling off colour. Been down in the mouth ever since you left. Not eating enough to keep a bird alive, and jumping out of her skin every time there's a knock on the door.'

Caroline's heart sank. This was scarcely the moment to be bringing the Comtesse news of further trouble. But there was no way to avoid the unpleasant task.

'I'm sorry to hear that, Jenks. You should have sent me word sooner. Will you let the Comtesse know I'm here?'

She sat down on one of the hall chairs while a footman was despatched to the Comtesse's private rooms. He was evidently ill-at-ease when he returned. He went up to Jenks, murmuring some message in a low voice. The butler approached Caroline reluctantly.

'I'm sorry, Miss,' he said. 'The Comtesse isn't feeling up to receiving visitors today. Could you call again another time? I'm sorry You've been put to all this trouble for nothing, Miss, but the Comtesse isn't herself these days, and that's a fact.'

She could not let Jenks see how frightened she felt. There was nothing he could do if the Comtesse refused to see her. She smiled at him as cheerfully as she could.

'I am glad to see that *you* are looking as robust as ever, Jenks.' The butler had been with the family for years and was accustomed to being teased about his well-padded corpulence. 'Please give the Comtesse my greetings and tell her that I hope we shall soon be able to spend an afternoon together.'

Jenks looked at her uneasily. 'There's not been any trouble has there, Miss?' He shuffled his feet, embarrassed at this departure from his normal dignified aloofness. 'Trouble for you, Miss, I was meaning.'

'I just came out on an impulse, Jenks. Everything . . . everything is going splendidly, thank you.'

She went through the open door quickly before he could think of any more awkward questions to ask, and ran down the steps with a fair imitation of light-hearted gaiety.

'We had better set out for my second port of call,' she said to the jarvey, making sure that Jenks could hear her words. 'Cavendish Square, driver, if you please.'

The jarvey obligingly asked no difficult questions. 'Yes, ma'am. Cavendish Square.' He climbed back up on to his perch, and Caroline saw, with a sigh of relief, that Jenks had gone back inside the house. Now she had only to cope with the problem finding herself a bed for the night. She doubted if any respectable hotel would take her without a maid or some other female companion.

The carriage stopped again. 'We're in Cavendish Square, ma'am,' said the jarvey. 'Which number was you wanting?'

Caroline stared at him blankly. She had called out the direction for no other reason than to deceive Jenks to her destination. Now she was here and she had no reason for staying. She could not, however, drive endlessly around the streets of London. For one thing, her slender purse would not stand the strain of meeting the cab-fare at the end of such a junket. With an effort she focused her attention upon the waiting driver. 'I don't know,' she said. 'That is to say, I have stupidly forgotten the number. I want the residence of the Dowager Baroness Carrisford. She lives in Cavendish Square.'

'I don't know her house, ma'am. But I'll ask. Somebody will know for sure.' He remounted the driver's seat and called out to an urchin waiting to sweep the crossing. 'Dowager Lady Carrisford, son. Which one's her 'ouse?'

As far as Caroline was concerned, the necessary directions were supplied far too quickly. It seemed no time at all before she was standing on the pavement outside an imposing entrance of white marble, her small bag resting forlornly on the curb beside her feet. She waited until the hackney-carriage and its cheerful driver were quite out of sight before mounting the first step leading to the porticoed entrance. She ran up the shallow flight of stairs, knowing that if she dragged her feet she would have time for second thoughts. She heard the bell pealing deep in the interior of the house and waited, with a pounding heart for the door to open.

A butler, looking remarkably like any other butler she had ever seen, opened the door and waited politely for her to state her business. His eyes flickered once over the incriminating piece of luggage, paused for an incredulous moment on her face, then stared politely but unseeingly into the middle distance. He was careful to avoid meeting her eyes.

'I would like to speak to Lady Carrisford,' said Caroline firmly. 'My name is Miss Adams.'

'Yes, Miss.' For one brief moment the

butler's gaze inadvertently encountered her own eyes. 'I know who you are, Miss.'

Caroline bit her lip nervously and stared abstractedly at the case stacked at her feet. To his lasting astonishment, the butler found himself stooping to pick it up.

'This way, Miss, if you please. I shall ascertain if her ladyship is at home.'

With the infallible judgment of a well-trained butler, he led her to a small, bare anteroom situated directly off the main entrance hall. A footman was loftily commanded to carry her bag into this same room. All the courtesies were thus observed, without committing the household to any inappropriate display of concern over a notorious young woman who arrived on the doorstep without a maid, and carrying her own baggage.

For the first ten minutes that she was kept waiting Caroline's nervousness mounted steadily, reaching a pitch at which communication with the Dowager, had she arrived, would have been impossible. Her throat had simply closed up and gave every evidence of never returning to active duty. During the next twenty minutes this paralysing fright gradually dissipated, leaving Caroline feeling numb and helpless. She was prey one minute to the conviction that she should get up and leave the house immediately, and prey the next minute to the equally strong conviction that she lacked the energy to move from her rigid and uncomfortable stance next to the potted fern which provided the room's single piece of ornamentation. But at the end of this half-hour wait, in a room containing neither chairs nor any method of heating, she discovered that her feelings of fright and helplessness had both dissolved into a powerful rage. If the Dowager intended to send her from the house, there was no need to keep her waiting half-an-hour to tell her so. If the Dowager intended to receive her then such a delay, without even a visit from a footman to provide a reason, was simply an example of appalling bad manners.

After a morning singularly lacking in food or drink, but amply provided with emotional drama, the feelings of rage rose to her head with the intoxicating effect of a brew of wine. Her pale complexion flushed with sudden colour, and her brown eyes were no longer misty with tears, but sparkling with temper. Caroline Adams was always, in any circumstances, a remarkably beautiful woman. In a rage, she acquired a tempestuous magnificence that set her apart from the merely beautiful.

She was on the point of leaving, furious with the world in general and herself in particular, when the Dowager finally entered the bleak little anteroom. The Dowager's eyes scanned her contemptuously, although some other emotion stirred unreadably in the depths of her gaze. Caroline raised her chin a little higher, and gave the Dowager Baroness back look for look. It was the Dowager who eventually broke the silence.

'The butler said it was you, but I couldn't believe him. You have a nerve, my girl, I will say that.'

Caroline spoke stiffly. 'I have come to ask your ladyship a favour.' In her angry mood the words came out without any hint of supplication. She swallowed hard. She had not meant to sound so aggressive.

The Dowager snorted. 'You don't think *I* am going to help one of my son's fancy women, do you? Disgraceful that you should force your way into my house. In my day you'd have been whipped at the car's tail, and that ain't no more than you deserve.'

'But *you* forced the introduction, my lady. It was you who came into our box at the theatre, not the other way around.' Caroline bit her lips in frustration. *This* was hardly the way to set about begging for employment.

'I don't have any control over Carrisford's actions,' said the Dowager impatiently, ignoring Caroline's interjection as if it had never been made. 'No good running to me if he's tired of you. If he hasn't pensioned you off handsomely, it'll be the first time.'

Caroline looked steadily at the Dowager and spoke very clearly and slowly. 'I was never your son's mistress, my lady. I was never any man's mistress. I have come to ask for your help in finding me some respectable employment. I will accept anything, anything at all, on condition that it will provide me with an honest living.'

The Dowager did not bother to conceal her amazement. 'Bit late in the day to be worrying about respectability, ain't it?'

'Yes,' said Caroline simply. 'That is why I have taken the desperate measure of throwing myself upon your charity, ma'am. Otherwise I fear . . . I fear there may not be much hope for me.'

'The cook needs a new assistant for peeling the vegetables and helping with the baking,' said the Dowager suddenly. 'Think you'd be any good at that?'

Caroline could not conceal the hope that flared in her eyes. 'I have little experience in a kitchen, ma'am, but I would be a very willing pupil, if you would only give me the chance to learn.'

The Dowager turned abruptly and started to walk out of the room. 'Follow me!' she commanded. 'Leave those silly cases.'

Caroline walked eagerly out of the room, perfectly willing to believe that the Dowager was personally escorting her to the kitchens. So great was her relief at the prospect of some job, however menial, that she did not pause to reflect upon the improbability of the Dowager Baroness concerning herself with appointments to the position of assistant-under-cook. She was bewildered when their brief walk ended inside a comfortable ground-floor sitting-room, amply provided with armchairs and rendered blessedly warm by a blazing log fire.

'Tell me about it,' Said the Dowager, settling herself into a chair close by the fire. 'Tell me what happened between you and my son.'

Caroline remained standing, although the armchairs by the fire looked more appealing by the second. 'I cannot tell you the truth, ma'am, so it is better if I do not spin you a tale that is half truth and half lies.' The hot colour invaded her cheeks. 'If you care to direct some questions to Lord Carrisford's housekeeper, I think she might be prepared to state that she believes me to be honest, ma'am. If I prove unsatisfactory at the job, you can easily dismiss me.'

'Sit down and stop talking nonsense,' said the Dowager sharply. 'You don't think anybody in their right mind would hire you to work in their kitchen, do you? You'd have every man-servant in the place fighting over you before the first night's meal was on the table.'

'Then what am I to do?' cried Caroline in desperation. 'It is not *fair* that I should be stigmatised because of the purely accidental arrangement of my features. No woman will hire me as a governess, no man believes in my virtue. Now you tell me that I may not even seek employment in a respectable kitchen. How am I to keep body and soul together if every honest means of procuring a livelihood is denied to me?'

'I am astonished that the thought of marriage has never occurred to you,' said the Dowager dryly.

Caroline was too distraught to answer diplomatically. 'Naturally, when I was younger, I expected to marry. But my circumstances have recently altered and I cannot expect to establish myself by marriage.' She fell silent as she thought of the one man whom she would marry with the greatest pleasure imaginable.

'Lift your head up and stop mumbling,' said the Dowager irritably. 'Why did you behave in such a vulgar fashion at the theatre? Talking all that nonsense about marrying my son.' Her shrewd eyes searched Caroline's features, reading the hesitancy of her expression. 'I'm not blind, you know, even if I am a bit hard of hearing. Carrisford looked at you as I've never seen him look at any other woman. Might as well have made love to you in the box, for it's what he was doing with his eyes.'

'It was all an act,' said Caroline bleakly. 'He is engaged upon an important mission for the government, ma'am, and it was necessary for him to pretend to be in love with me.'

A strange barking sound escaped from the Dowager, and Caroline realised it was a cackle of laughter. 'Mighty convenient government work that requires a man to sit and moon at the feet of the most beautiful female to hit London in a decade.'

In her agitation, Caroline sprang to her feet and strode restlessly around the room. It was probably fortunate that she could not hear the desolation which tinged her next words. 'Believe me, ma'am, there were circumstances that made such a pretence necessary. Lord Carrisford does not even like me. He has never made the slightest effort to disguise his true feelings for me. He would never have spent time with me had it not been for his position as adviser to Lord Liverpool. He d-dislikes me, ma'am. I do not think he considers me at all beautiful now that he has become accustomed to having me about the house.'

Since she was much occupied in twisting her best lace handkerchief into an unrecognisable shred of limp rag, she failed to observe the suddenly arrested attention of the Dowager's wandering gaze. 'Who are your parents, gal, and where did Carrisford meet you?' asked the Dowager.

Caroline saw no reason for concealment. 'My father was Colonel Adams of the Fourth Foot, ma'am, and my mother was the only child of Sir Henry Beecham. Both families live in Yorkshire, ma'am.'

'And you met Carrisford . . . ?'

'My stepmother is the Comtesse de la Rivière,' said Caroline defiantly. 'She runs a gambling establishment in Mount Street and I helped her in the card-rooms. Lord Carrisford met me there.'

'If you expect me to believe that Carrisford, having met you working at the tables in a gambling-house, made no push to set you up as his mistress, then you are missing your mark, my girl. One look at you would be quite sufficient to make him determined to have you. Don't expect me to help you if you are going to try and palm me off with that sort of farradiddle.'

Caroline's handkerchief suffered a further degree of disintegration. 'Lord Carrisford did make me an offer, ma'am. He was not the first to do so, of course, but he was undoubtedly the most offensive. He rated his own attractions sufficiently highly that he saw no difficulty in establishing me as his mistress, other than inducing me to be reasonable about the terms.' The angry sparkle in Caroline's eyes faded, and her voice died away unhappily. 'I cannot *altogether* blame him for such an assumption.'

'It was the power of his purse which he rated so high, you know,' said the Dowager briskly. 'He has learned to have a cynical respect for the size of his personal fortune. Anyway, that is beside the point. One minute he is propositioning you, unsuccessfully according to you. The next moment you are living in his house but you're not his mistress and, according to you, he don't even notice you're beautiful any more.'

'It sounds ridiculous, I know. But there are other people involved in my story, ma'am, and I am not at liberty to reveal the precise circumstances of my arrangement with Lord Carrisford. When I refused to become his mistress on any terms whatsoever he lost interest in me as a woman. If it had not been for the special circumstances of my family he would never have pursued the liaison.' She could not conceal the pain in her voice. 'I may not have lived up to Lord Carrisford's expectations as a potential mistress, but he has found me a uniquely useful tool in every other respect.'

'So why didn't you become his mistress when you had the chance? From all I hear, he's a generous provider and you *are* in love with him I gather?'

Caroline regarded the Dowager in stricken silence. She had not realised her feelings were so painfully transparent. She walked towards the door. 'You would not think to address such a question to one of your friends' daughters, ma'am, so I cannot think why you choose to ask it of me. My upbringing and moral scruples make such a rôle abhorrent to me, whatever my feelings about the man in question.'

'My friends' daughters aren't usually seen sitting in my son's box, with their arms and necks strung about with more jewels than a jeweller's window. I do not think my question was unreasonable.' The Dowager scarcely paused to draw breath. 'Perhaps you would like to stay with me for a few days. As my guest. Lucinda's babbling about going back to stay with her brother, and it will make a pleasant change to have a pretty face across the dinner-table.'

Hope and a sense of duty warred within Caroline. Resolutely, she squashed the flicker of hope. 'You must not offer me hospitality, ma'am. I have no reputation left and you know nothing about me.'

'On the contrary, I know a deal more about you than I do about most of the drab females aspiring to catch Carrisford's attention. Besides, I haven't had such a splendid opportunity to annoy my family for years.'

'The last few weeks have provided me with a surfeit of acting as somebody's else's instrument of revenge.'

'Pish, pash, girl. You are scarce in a position to quibble over details. Save your opposition until you find out how we go along. I ain't made up my mind what I shall do with you exactly.' She looked shrewdly at Caroline. 'If I were you, I should eat and sleep before making any grand moral gestures. Devilish fatiguing to be moral on an empty stomach.'

Caroline could not help giving a small smile. 'You are, regrettably, quite right, ma'am. I fear my nature is not easily adapted to constant sessions of high drama. I should not accept your kind offer of hospitality, but I am sorely tempted to so so.'

'Then it's settled,' said the Dowager, giving a vigorous tug at the bell-pull and being rewarded by the instant appearance of a footman. 'Masters, take Miss Adams' baggage to the Rose Room.' She turned back to Caroline. 'It's a dreadful room. Looks as though the painter had been dreaming of cabbages the night before he started painting. But you'll be comfortable there. Ask the maids to bring you some luncheon on a tray. Dinner's at six. Can't stand these newfangled eating habits where you have to wait until breakfast-time tomorrow before it's time to eat dinner tonight.'

Caroline fixed her regard steadily upon the Dowager's wrinkled face. 'I am deeply grateful to your ladyship. If there is ever any opportunity for me to express my gratitude in some way, I beg you will let me know.'

'I shan't hesitate to do so,' said the Dowager. 'Enjoy your rest, and think how pleasant it is to look forward to dinner, knowing you ain't required to peel the vegetables.'

Chapter Thirteen

THE Dowager Baroness Carrisford was no great believer in the value of exercise. She doubted its beneficial effects upon the general state of her constitution and actively disliked the discomforts attendant upon its practice. She therefore prepared herself to make a morning call with the meticulous attention to personal comfort that others might have expended for a three-week journey to the Outer Hebrides.

On the morning after Caroline's arrival in her household, she announced that she would make a journey across town to call upon her son. Her servants, well used to the elaborate routine preceding the Dowager's most minor excursions, bore up remarkably well under the string of conflicting orders issuing from their mistress's lips, and it took no more than an hour and a half before the servants succeeded in removing the Dowager from the breakfast-table and installing her, well-wrapped and cushioned, in the recesses of her barouche. The Dowager, much to the servants' relief, appeared to be in a particularly good humour, suffering several minor mishaps with no more than a brief bark of disapproval, soon forgotten.

There was more space inside the carriage than was usual, since the Dowager was accompanied only by her personal maid. Cousin Lucinda, the unfortunate relative of uncertain age who was normally expected to keep the Dowager company and prevent the Dowager's more outrageous plans for amusement, had been left behind to pack her bag. Poor Cousin Lucinda, unable to believe the evidence of her maiden eyes when she had found Caroline (That Woman) seated across from her at the dinner-table, was now preparing herself for a long journey to join her brother, an elderly bishop of unimpeachable propriety and High Tory sentiments. Nothing, Lucinda had informed the Dowager in tragic accents, would prevail upon her to remain in a household where females of That Sort were permitted to partake of the family dinner. The Dowager, who had accepted the news of her companion's departure with the most unflattering appearance of equanimity, now settled back against the cushions of the barouche with a general air of contentment. The maid, a veteran of twenty years' service, wondered what devilment the old termagant was up to this time.

Lord Carrisford, whose own black mood was far removed from the self-satisfaction exhibited by his mother, wondered much the same thing when Atkins came into the library bearing news of the Dowager's arrival. Carrisford nodded a reluctant agreement to receive his mother, and put down his pen with a sigh. He had been writing instructions and messages since seven o'clock in the morning and had spent yesterday fruitlessly scouring the town for a trace of Caroline, so he was tired enough to welcome a moment's break in his work. He felt little enthusiasm for an acrimonious encounter with his mother, however, and shrank for the thought that his raw and tumultuous feelings about Caroline might, of necessity, be exposed to the lash of his mother's sarcastic tongue.

It was evident that the Dowager was on the attack from the moment of her entrance into the library.

'Nice day,' she said, making her single concession to the usual courtesies. 'You look shockin'. Not at all the thing.' She peered round the library with spurious interest. 'Where's your fancy woman, or do you only bring her out at night? Probably wise. Doubt if her complexion would stand examination in the light of day. They never do.'

Lord Carrisford gritted his teeth. The Dowager, as he knew from long experience, was virtually unmanageable in this sort of mood.

'Please sit down, Mama. I believe the green chair is tolerably comfortable for people of advanced years. May I send for some refreshments?'

The Dowager disposed herself in the green chair, rustling the faded satin of her mourning-clothes until she was fully satisfied with the comfort of her position. 'I just had breakfast,' she said, cheerfully ignoring her son's grim expression. 'When I saw the sun, I decided to come out for a drive and where better—for a person of my advanced years—where better, I thought, than to come and see you. Who could be happier to see me than my eldest son, the heir to everything I hold dear?'

'Very touching,' said Lord Carrisford resignedly. 'Well, Mama, we both know that you have come here to be as aggravating as you know how to be. The only question is whether or not you are prepared to save us both some time by coming immediately to the point of your visit. I would appreciate it if you could express your purpose within the next few minutes or so.' He gestured to the mound of papers tumbling across his desk. 'As you can see, I am very busy this morning.'

The Dowager obligingly stared at the piles of paper. 'You're a strange man,' she said in a tone of voice which suggested such strangeness was praiseworthy or, at the very least, inevitable. 'Positively depressing in the way you assume responsibility for Lord Liverpool and his collection of imbeciles at the War Office. And no sense of responsibility at all when it comes to your own family.'

'Ah!' said Lord Carrisford. 'I see we are to come right to it. I am certain you have no interest in discussing my responsibilities to Lord Liverpool, so I suppose you are here to discuss some mythical breach of my responsibility to the family?'

'Hardly mythical, Richard,' cut in the Dowager promptly. 'You are five-and-thirty, you know, which is several years past the time when you should start thinking about providing a Carrisford heir.' Just for an instant her voice softened with a hint of warm concern. 'It is eight years since Elizabeth Petrie died, my dear. You cannot mourn for ever. If she were here she would be the first to tell you so.'

'You are labouring under a misapprehension, Mama,' said Lord Carrisford. 'When Elizabeth died only weeks before our marriage was due to take place I was very sorry. But life goes on, and my life has been very full. It has been circumstances, rather than inconsolable grief, which kept me single.' He looked at his mother in sudden irritation. 'Dammit, Mama! Why am I defending my actions to you? I have two healthy brothers who are both married, and Christopher has already produced three sons of his own. You cannot pretend that I must hurry to the altar in order to preserve the Carrisford name.'

'Christopher married Letty Bishop,' said the Dowager obscurely. 'All the boys look just like her. Act like her too.'

Lord Carrisford had no difficulty in following his mother's meaning. 'Yes, well, it is undoubtedly unfortunate that the boys don't take after Chris, and I do not relish the thought of Letty's offspring stepping into my shoes. But Good God, ma'am, I am five-and thirty, not five-and-fifty! I do not feel that my capacity for producing sons is altogether past.'

'True,' said the Dowager. 'But it would be so much more desirable if they were legitimate.'

Lord Carrisford gave an exclamation of annoyance. 'Mama, I know quite well what has precipitated this visit of yours, and I must tell you that I am not in the mood to receive one of your scolds today. I am exceptionally busy. A matter which has occupied my attention for the past several months is at any moment likely to come to a point of crisis. I am awaiting messengers from France, Lord Liverpool delivers hourly notes begging for my opinion, a young *émigré*, at my request, is risking the life of his father, and *you* wish to beguile an idle morning by quarrelling over the woman you discovered with me at the theatre last week. Well, ma'am, I do not have time to humour you. You may deliver your lectures at some other time. In the meantime, it will no doubt give you considerable pleasure to learn that the woman in question has left my protection. I trust you are now satisfied and will see fit to leave me to pursue my official business in peace.'

'You are extraordinarily touchy about such a trivial matter,' said the Dowager. 'If you are tired of whatever-her-name was, it is undoubtedly better that you got rid of her. Now you are free to turn your attention to some of the eminently suitable girls whom you might wish to make your bride. What about the eldest Greenaway girl? She's got blond hair like what's-her-name. Curly, too.'

Lord Carrisford fell into the trap. 'You cannot be meaning Julia Greenaway? To compare her frizzed straw with Caroline's hair is like comparing a hayfield to spun gold. Not to mention the fact that two minutes of Miss Greenaway's company is sufficient to drive me to distraction, whereas with Caroline . . .' He stopped at the sight of the Dowager's smirk of satisfaction. 'Very well,' he snapped. 'You have achieved your purpose. You shall hear it. Caroline has left my protection, it is true, but not because I wished her to do so. There was a misunderstanding. I did not ask her to go, and the worst of it is, I am responsible for her in a way you cannot be expected to understand. The circumstances of our relationship are not what they appear.' He looked grimly at his mother. 'That, however, is entirely my affair, and I have not the slightest intention of allowing you to poke your enterprising nose any further into my business. So you may as well go home. You will learn nothing further from me.'

'I have already heard quite enough,' said the Dowager, rising to her feet and retieing the ribbons of her bonnet in a lop-sided bow. 'Now where did I put my reticule? So inconvenient that I had to leave the maid sitting outside. But it's never possible To have a conversation with you that's fit for a servant's ears.'

'That,' said Lord Carrisford in forbidding accents, 'is certainly not by my choice.' He suddenly remembered Cousin Lucinda, who usually accompanied his mother on her morning visits. 'Good Lord! You have surely never left that poor cousin of yours sitting outside in the hallway all this time?'

'Cousin Lucinda is at home packing,' said the Dowager absently. 'She feels it is time for another visit to the Bishop. I have a new companion. She's not here. You must come and meet her some time.'

'That is indeed a treat to look forward to. Your companions are noted for their vivacity and charm.'

'Yes,' said the Dowager. 'I am going to the theatre with her this evening. You may join us.'

'My affairs are unlikely to permit me to indulge in frivolous entertainments, ma'am.'

'Oh lord, there's nothing frivolous about it. They're doing "Hamlet" again. You can be miserable all evening and come away before the farce to make quite sure that you feel you've been doing nothing but your duty. I shall expect you, Richard. I am an old woman, and cannot count on making many more junkets up to London. This may be your last chance to escort me to the play.'

Lord Carrisford gave a vigorous tug at the bell-rope. 'You, dear lady, will be going to plays long after I am confined to a bath-chair. Atkins!' He greeted the appearance of the butler with unfeigned relief. 'Please escort her ladyship back to her carriage. Goodbye, Mama.' Ruthlessly he turned back to his papers.

'Goodness, Richard, you are sadly out of sorts this morning. I shall look forward to seeing you at the theatre tonight. I hope you will be in a better temper by then.'

She went quickly out of the room before he could discover further reasons to protest, and joined her maid with her face wreathed in smiles. 'We can go home now,' she said cheerfully. 'That was a *very* satisfactory visit.'

Lord Carrisford had written no more than three or four sentences of his latest memorandum to the War Ministry when Atkins again appeared at the bookroom door. 'There are two more visitors, m'lord. I have taken the liberty of conducting them to the Chinese room.'

'Who are they?' Lord Carrisford asked quickly.

'It is the Count de la Rivière and the Dowager Countess, m'lord.'

Lord Carrisford went swiftly along the corridor to the small sitting-room, unable to shake of the uncomfortable memories of his last visit to the room.

'What news?' he asked eagerly, as soon as he had greeted the Comtesse and her son. 'Has she sent you word?'

Philippe paced in agitation up and down the room. 'There has been nothing, my lord. Nothing since Jenks sent her away yesterday at noon. Where can she have gone? She has no friends she could turn to, and God knows if she has any money. *Mon Dieu!* How could I have spoken to her so, when I have known the value of her character for years!'

The Comtesse was very pale, but she was more in control of herself than her son. 'Have you sent enquiries to Harrogate, my lord?'

'I have sent an express, but it could be a week before we have a reply. We cannot assume she has gone there and make no other push to discover her whereabouts. I have examined her wardrobe, and it seems to me that she has taken very few clothes. I cannot understand how she left the house without any of the servants becoming aware of her plans. In the middle of the day, as well.'

'Have you questioned *all* the servants?' asked the Comtesse.

'I have spoken to the footmen on duty at the time she left, and I have asked Atkins if he knows anything. Perhaps I should question the housekeeper personally. She may not have told Atkins all that she knows.' He stopped talking as the butler entered the room carrying a tray of madeira and several wine-glasses. 'Ask Bessie to come here, will you, Atkins?'

As soon as the butler had withdrawn the Comtesse spoke again. 'As regards the other matter, my lord, the night has certainly brought wisdom. Philippe and I were foolish not to bring word of our dilemma to you once we knew how intimately involved you were. But the threat hanging over our heads is a grave one. It is not easy to take an action which may threaten the life of somebody most dear.'

Lord Carrisford replied calmly, his level tones seeming to reassure even Philippe, who stopped his restless pacing and concentrated his attention upon Lord Carrisford. 'From my experience of previous incidents, Madame, I think it is only fair to warn you that I personally doubt very much if your husband is still alive.'

The Comtesse turned even paler than before. 'You mean . . . you mean, the Bonapartists suspect our loyalty and have killed him?'

'No, Madame. No such thing. But I have heard of at least one similar incident where the same kind of ploy was used. Records from the time of the Terror are incomplete, so it is the easiest thing in the world to select a family which, for some reason, can be of use to the Imperial cause, and then to trick that family into believing they must co-operate with the Bonapartists or some loved one will die. In your own case, the French government saw how André de la Rivière could be used to feed false information to the British military authorities. It was, however, necessary to ensure that nobody on this side of the Channel should dispute the claims of the false count. It was necessary for you, Madame, to remain silent and for Philippe's claims to be dismissed. The French conceived the excellent idea of naming Philippe to me as a Bonapartist agent, thus ensuring that I would view all his actions with the utmost suspicion.'

'The ploy was almost successful,' said Philippe wryly.

'More than you yet realise,' said Lord

Carrisford. 'But it is my own personal conviction that your husband died in the executions of the Terror, just as you have always believed. Napoleon's agents resurrected him simply as a means of ensuring your co-operation. The same trick was used against the Vicomte d'Arles, except that it was his son who supposedly languished in gaol.'

'So what are we to do now, my lord?' asked Philippe.

'You will need to do very little,' said Lord Carrisford. 'As far as M. Patin is concerned, you and the Comtesse have done all that can be expected.'

'Patin is even pleased at the frequent contacts between us,' said Philippe. 'He believes I conspired to introduce Caroline into your household expressly to keep watch over you.'

'Don't disillusion him, I beg. From the point of view of the British government, it is better if M. Patin and his fellow conspirators do not learn that their plot is discovered. So long as they believe that I'm acting on André's false information, we can plan safely on doing virtually the opposite of what he recommends.'

The Comtesse, who had evidently been

pursuing her own train of thought, could not conceal the anxiety which wracked her.

'But what of my husband, my lord? How shall we even find out if he is dead or alive? To wonder for the rest of my life if I have betrayed him—that is too much!'

'Don't give up hope of discovering the truth, Madame. We have informants operating actually inside the prisons. If he is alive we shall hear of it. Besides, M. Patin set a trap for his own feet when he swore to you that your husband is imprisoned in Mont-Saint-Michel. If he is not there I think you can safely assume that he isn't held anywhere. I believe, Madame, that you will find out eventually that your husband rests in peace, beyond the reach of Napoleon and his agents.'

'I pray God you are correct. To have spent twenty years in a revolutionary prison is a punishment nobody should have to endure. Death my husband could meet proudly. Imprisonment would be virtually impossible for a man of his temperament.'

Lord Carrisford led her gently to a seat by the fire. 'Come, Madame. I am forgetful of my manners this morning. Sit here and take some wine and put these troublesome thoughts out of your mind for a little while.

I have one more matter to discuss with Philippe, and then we can feel free to turn our attention to the problem of Caroline's whereabouts.' He poured out two glasses of madeira. 'M. le Comte, will you join us? I have one further point to make with you . . .'

He broke off at the sound of a tap on the panels of the door. 'Ah, Bessie, you have arrived at last!' he said. 'Please come in. I wish to ask you some questions about Miss Adams.'

'Yes, my lord.'

'I was not expecting Miss Adams to leave when she did, and I am anxious to get in touch with her. Did she confide her destination to you?'

'No, my lord.'

Lord Carrisford tried again. 'I am anxious to ascertain that no harm had befallen Miss Adams. That is very difficult to do when I am unable to discover where she has gone.'

'Very difficult, my lord.'

Lord Carrisford's patience gave away. 'I've endured your uncomfortable ways, Bessie, for the last thirty years. When my father was alive I had no choice. But I no longer have to tolerate insubordination from a servant in my own household. Unless you tell me what you know about Miss Adams' departure from here I shall take great delight in pensioning you off from my service. You will then be at liberty to dedicate all your time to the salvation of erring mankind, and I shall be at liberty to conduct my life in the manner I see fit. Do I make myself plain?'

'Yes, my lord.' After one glance at Lord Carrisford's thunderous brow, Bessie continued hastily. 'But I can't tell you anything much, because Miss Adams didn't tell me where she was going. She said what I didn't know I wouldn't have to conceal. She took a small case with her and asked me to let her out of the servants' entrance. She picked up a hackney at the end of the street and that's all I know.'

The Comtesse shook her head despairingly. 'She came to my house and I, thinking it was no more than a social call, sent her away again because I was being watched by M. Patin. Where she went from my house we have no idea.'

Lord Carrisford spoke sternly. 'Very well, Bessie, you may leave us. But if you do have word from Miss Adams I wish to hear of it.'

Bessie curtsied in chastened silence and withdrew from the room.

'No wonder I long for the peaceful life of the Peninsula,' said Lord Carrisford. 'There I had only a half-dozen foreign princes and a few hundred British soldiers to worry about, and none of them had ever heard of Charles Wesley. If only my father had not been such a virtuous man! His servants are such a depressingly virtuous legacy.'

Philippe stepped forward with ill-concealed impatience. 'There was one further matter to discuss with me, my lord. Could we deal with it at once? I am anxious to pursue my enquiries as to my sister's whereabouts.'

'Oh yes,' said Lord Carrisford. 'There *is* one further matter. I am afraid, *M. le Comte,* that I shall have to ask you to accompany me to the Tower. I have a warrant here for your arrest on a charge of treason.'

Chapter Fourteen

AN excellent dinner and a long night's rest combined to restore Caroline's normal state of robust good sense, and in the clear light of morning she realised that there was not a shred of justification for accepting the Dowager's offer of employment. Having reached this sensible conclusion, she quickly repacked her small valise before her resolution could weaken once again. She then set about preparing herself mentally for the journey to Harrogate, and for a difficult session with the Dowager before she left.

The Dowager, unfortunately, was not in the house, and Caroline was compelled to pass an anxious morning waiting for her benefactor's return. Her determination to leave did not waiver, although her regrets increased with the passage of every hour. Luncheon had long since passed before the Dowager finally returned to the house and indicated that she would see Caroline.

The interview, at least as far as Caroline was concerned, quite failed to achieve its purpose. The Dowager simply refused to listen to her new companion, and would not agree that there was any reason whatsoever for Caroline to travel to Harrogate.

'I am beginning to wonder if Lord Carrisford is not right,' Caroline exclaimed in exasperation. 'Persuading you to change your mind, ma'am, is a more difficult task than holding back the River Thames in flood.'

'Very true,' said the Dowager, pleased at the compliment. 'Since I am invariably right in my decisions, I have never so far seen any reason to change my mind. It is useless for others to oppose me. Only see how correct I was in my judgment about you!' She paused to draw breath, then changed the subject abruptly. 'Got any evening-clothes with you? Proper ones, I mean, not that dreary thing you wore last night.'

Caroline replied with great dignity. 'When I left Carrisford House, ma'am, I selected two gowns which I felt would be appropriate to my new station in life. I wore one of them last night. I have the other one with me. It is also grey.'

'I'd throw them away if I were you,' said the Dowager. 'Don't make you look one bit less beautiful. Just makes people wonder how you'd look if you were properly fitted out. I'll send over to Carrisford House and tell them to deliver your clothes here.'

'Oh no, ma'am! I beg you will not.' She stopped in some confusion. 'Forgive me, ma'am, but I would much prefer to keep my whereabouts secret.'

'Why?'

'Why?' Caroline repeated the question blankly. 'Well, ma'am, it is because . . . That is to say . . .'

'You can't hide from Carrisford for the rest of your life. Bound to bump into him sooner or later. You may meet him anywhere, you know. He's received by a score of people who should know better.'

Caroline twisted her hands despairingly. 'You cannot be serious in your determination to keep me as your companion, ma'am. Only think of how many people must have seen me at the theatre with Lord Carrisford! And those who did not see me personally have undoubtedly heard exaggerated stories of what transpired.'

The Dowager's cackle erupted from deep in her throat. 'That is why we are going back to Covent Garden tonight. It'll be worth a year of your salary just to see some of their faces when we walk into my box together.'

Caroline stood up and spoke with as much dignity as she could muster. 'Diverting for you, ma'am, no doubt, but considerably less entertaining for me. I do not find it easy to be the cynosure of all eyes.'

'Don't be more of a fool than you need, girl. Come to the theatre with me and your

238

reputation is restored to you at a single stroke. Ain't that worth a few stares?' She did not allow Caroline to speak, but swept on imperiously. 'What are your plans for this afternoon?'

'I must visit my stepmother's house,' said Caroline. 'She does not know where I am and may be worried.'

'I'll send one of the footmen to inform her,' said the Dowager, who seemed reluctant to let Caroline out of her sight.

'It is necessary for me to go myself,' said Caroline. 'Naturally, I would not dream of troubling your coachman, so I shall take a hackeny.'

'You'll do no such thing. Most unsuitable method of conveyance for a young female. I shall come with you, since you insist upon going.'

Caroline could hardly object to an offer which, coming from anybody else, would have seemed a courteous gesture. She suspected the Dowager's motives and was annoyed that she would not easily be able to converse privately with her stepmother. She was determined to snatch a few minutes alone with the Comtesse, even if it proved necessary to be rude to the Dowager. Caroline was beginning to suspect that the only way to handle her new employer was to display a ruthlessness every bit as great as the Dowager's own.

For the time being Caroline was content to smile acceptance of the Dowager's offer and to enquire politely how soon they might set out. The Dowager, whose energy was unfailing when devoted to the noble cause of interfering in other people's concerns, indicated graciously that she was perfect agreeable to setting out at once.

It was therefore still early in the afternoon when the Dowager's carriage halted outside No. 10 Mount Street. Jenks, who was much impressed by the imposing crests painted on the door-panels, was very sorry that he had to turn such important callers away. However, the Comtesse really was out of the house and, since she had given no indication when she might return, there was no point in suggesting that the callers should come inside and wait.

It was impossible for Caroline to conceal her chagrin when told that the Comtesse was once again unavailable. Jenks, who had always felt a particular soft spot for the beautiful Miss Adams, relented his hauteur of manner sufficiently to ask if the visitors would care to step into the drawing-room and write a message for the Comtesse.

'The Countess de la Rivière is nowhere in the house, Miss Adams,' he said. He eyed the formidable figure of the Dowager somewhat doubtfully, but in the end decided to confess the full horror of the situation. 'Due to a regrettable misunderstanding, Miss, it seems that Monsewer Philippe has been apprehended. The Countess is endeavouring to set matters right, which is why she is not at home this afternoon.'

'Apprehended?' Fear twisted Caroline's stomach muscles into a tight knot. 'You cannot mean that he has been arrested?'

Jenks nodded gloomily. 'The Countess de la Rivière informed me that a warrant for his arrest was issued by Lord Liverpool's office. Monsewer Philippe is in the Tower of London,' he said, unable to conceal a ghoulish relish at the awfulness of his news.

'Oh dear heaven!' Caroline turned so pale that both Jenks and the Dowager clutched her arms, convinced that she was about to faint.

'I shouldn't ought to have told you, Miss,' said Jenks remorsefully. 'Would you come inside and take a glass of ratafia, Miss? It's what the Countess would wish, I'm sure.'

241

Caroline paid no attention whatsoever to this helpful suggestion, but turned and ran blindly down the shallow flight of stairs. 'Carrisford House!' she commanded the astonished coachman as she panted up to the barouche. 'At once!'

'If you don't mind, Miss, I'd prefer to wait until the Dowager Baroness is inside her own carriage before I drive off.'

The Dowager arrived beside the coach at this inauspicious moment and allowed the groom to hand her inside. Caroline turned to her contritely.

'I'm sorry, ma'am. I'm afraid that my anger and fright were so great I temporarily forgot my manners.'

The Dowager spoke briskly. 'You want to go to Carrisford House? I shall come with you.'

'Thank you, ma'am. But I beg you not to ask me any questions.'

'You cannot expect me not to be curious,' said the Dowager reasonably. 'Your stepbrother has been sent to prison and you immediately go flying off and order my coachman to make you to Richard's house. *Anybody* would be interested, and I am not just anybody.'

'Indeed not, ma'am,' said Caroline with

wry agreement. Her temper was back under control again now, and she had merely to cope with a corroding sensation of disillusion. By concentrating all her thoughts upon the plight of her stepbrother, she was able to do a tolerable job of repressing the misery she felt at Lord Carrisford's perfidy. Even now, despite all the evidence, she could hardly reconcile her knowledge of Carrisford's character with the heartless betrayal of a very young, and very confused young man. Philippe was at most an unwilling pawn in a game not of his own devising, and she had believed Lord Carrisford would see this as clearly as she did herself. Philippe needed the aid of an older and wiser man, not punishment for struggling to cope with a moral dilemma too great for him to resolve alone. Her hands clenched involuntarily at the unwelcome memory of her own part in Philippe's betrayal and its bitter aftermath. She did not realise that her cheeks paled at the recollection, for she was staring blindly out of the carriage window. Never had such a short journey seemed to take so long.

'You seem quite certain that Richard can bring some light to bear on this situation,' said the Dowager.

'Since he alone is responsible for my stepbrother's incarceration, I imagine he could use his influence to secure Philippe's release,' said Caroline.

'One would think so,' said the Dowager. She looked at Caroline's tightly-controlled features and said with remarkable gentleness, 'Richard will have done nothing to harm your stepbrother, my dear. Unless it was deserved, of course.'

It was obviously impossible to refute this statement without a further breach of manners, so Caroline contented herself with remarking, 'No, ma'am,' and then relapsed into unhappy silence until the footman appeared at the carriage door and let down the steps.

In other circumstances she might have managed to derive a certain amount of merriment from the sight of Atkins' ill-concealed amazement when he opened the door and observed his master's supposed mistress arm-in-arm with his master's mother. As it was, Caroline felt hard pushed to conceal her impatience as the butler greeted the Dowager with ponderous dignity at the same time as he tried hard not to stare at Caroline. The initial courtesies over, however, he obviously abandoned the futile attempt to disguise his bewilderment, and his gaze crept round to fasten upon Caroline's face. His mouth formed a small circle of astonishment, and he lapsed into silence.

'Well, is Lord Carrisford in?' asked the Dowager. 'Are you planning to keep us standing on the doorstep all afternoon while you find out?'

Recalled to a sense of his duties, the butler dragged his eyes away from Miss Adams and offered to escort the ladies into the drawing-room for some refreshment. 'But I regret to say, my lady, that the master is not at home. He left the house before noon and is not planning to return until this evening.' He coughed delicately. 'He is absent on government business, you understand, my lady. He is conferring with Lord Liverpool concerning a young traitor what was arrested in this very house yesterday. Terrible the ingratitude of the foreigners who come here expecting us to take them in and make them welcome.'

'Arrested here! Then it is as I thought. *He* is responsible for my brother's imprisonment. Why, oh why, did I not shoot him when I had the chance? *He* is the traitor!'

The Dowager did not venture to comment upon these rhetorical questions and, by the exercise of superhuman self-control, even managed to refrain from asking just when Caroline had previously felt moved to shoot Lord Carrisford. She smiled brightly at the butler, whose jaw appeared to have dropped permanently open, and patted Caroline gently upon the arm.

'Just so, my dear. I have *frequently* thought that his character would have been much improved by the more diligent use of a horsewhip. Pistols are so very final, don't you think? But his father enjoyed the temperament of a saint and insisted that our children would all be adequately trained by the use of kind words and reasonable explanations. So unfortunate that my dear husband never realised that children don't have an ounce of reasonableness in their entire body. Please don't forget to remind Lord Carrisford that he has promised to join me at the theatre tonight. Covent Garden.'

Caroline looked justifiably startled at the strange conclusion to the Dowager's speech. The butler, older and wiser in his ways, simply bowed politely and said that he would make sure Lord Carrisford was given the message.

The butler watched the two ladies depart down the flight of marble stairs, and wished he could have been a fly on the inside wall of the barouche. Miss Adams (grudgingly he promoted her in his thoughts from That Woman, since the Dowager had chosen to give her countenance) was in a devil of a temper or he missed his guess. And she looked as if she might be one of the few people, male or female, capable of giving the Old Lady almost as good as she got. Atkins closed the front door with a sigh of regret. It was a pity the master hadn't been home. An encounter between those three characters would have been well worth watching.

Chapter Fifteen

CAROLINE walked slowly down the imposing main staircase of the Dowager's townhouse. Her eyes were fixed upon the bouquet of rosebuds she carried in her hands, but in her mind's eye she saw nothing save the grim stone walls of a prison cell. The memory of her brother's final, hate-filled outburst ate like acid into her heart, leaving her with no peace and no will to resist the Dowager's determination that they should both go to Covent Garden.

Her clothes had arrived earlier from Carrisford House, but she had felt no interest in this sudden replenishment of her wardrobe and had stood in listless silence as the Dowager's personal maid bustled around the room, making small exclamations of satisfaction as she dressed her charge. If called upon to describe the dress she was wearing, Caroline would have been unable even to name the colour without glancing down to refresh her memory.

She did not see that the Dowager already waited for her at the foot of the stairs, nor did she hear the tiny gasp that emerged from the Dowager's lips. Even when her mind was concentrating upon the matters directly at hand, Caroline tended to forget the effect her appearance could have upon the people around her. The Dowager, who had so far seen Caroline dressed either in drab morning-clothes, or decked out to play the rôle of an expensive Cyprian, was forced to blink once or twice to convince herself that the pale vision descending the stairs was composed of flesh and blood. Caroline was wearing a simple gown of white silk, her sole ornaments the fresh flowers woven into her hair and carried in her hands. She presented a picture of ethereal beauty rarely seen outside the gilded frame of a painter's dream world. The Dowager's gasp was quickly smothered in a sigh of considerable satisfaction.

Their conversation during the journey to the theatre was desultory in the extreme and almost entirely devoid of any particle of sense. Caroline did rouse herself long enough to reflect that her worry over Philippe and her bitterness towards Lord Carrisford combined to produce at least one desirable effect: their outing to the theatre, and the knowledge that she would once again be exposed to the interested speculation of an entire audience, no longer worried her. How could she feel concern over such trivia when her entire being ached with a painful mixture of fear, resentment and love? These, unfortunately, were not thoughts she could share with the Dowager, so she talked determinedly of the weather and stared out of the carriage window when even this topic finally failed her.

Her splendid sense of protective isolation cracked somewhat when they entered the Dowager's box, and she endeavoured to sit down as much in the shadows as possible. For one moment it seemed that every eye in the house was turned upon them, and for a few devastating seconds the hum of conversation faded away into utter silence. Caroline raised her chin a little higher and moved her chair closer to the Dowager's.

'The theatre seems rather thin of company this evening,' she remarked as she gave a convincing performance of gazing round the audience. In actual fact, she would not have noticed if the audience had been spilling over into the aisles, and the Dowager probably guessed as much.

However, the Dowager smiled in an amicable fashion. 'Just what I thought myself,' she said. She reached out and touched Caroline lightly on the arm, exhibiting a brief flash of her son's captivating charm of manner. 'Good gal!' she said. 'I knew you could do it.'

They did not exchange any further conversation, since the Dowager was much occupied in bowing and smiling to as many of her friends as she could manage to spy, and Caroline was more than content to be left alone with the turmoil of her private thoughts. The play was well advanced before her attention was finally turned to the actors upon the stage. She was surprised to discover that they were watching a performance of 'Hamlet'. She thought ruefully that she was appropriately dressed for the occasion. Ophelia, if she remembered correctly, was much addicted to virginal white clothes and to the strewing of flowers although only after she had been driven mad by hopeless love. Caroline felt her mouth twitch into a small smile and was relieved to discover that she still remembered how to laugh at herself. Cheered by the realisation that she was not yet sunk totally into maudlin sentimentality, she resolved to behave with great propriety during the interval.

This was an excellent resolution, and might even have been adhered to had the end of the first act not happened to coincide with the entrance of Lord Carrisford. He strode into his mother's box and nodded his head briefly at the maid.

'Wait outside,' he ordered curtly.

He raised his mother's hand to his lips and said through clenched teeth, 'I might have expected to find you behind this latest piece of interference!'

'Your manners, Carrisford, leave a great deal to be desired,' said the Dowager coldly. 'May I present to you my new companion? Lord Carrisford. Miss Caroline Adams.'

Lord Carrisford turned a burning gaze

upon Caroline's pale face. 'We have met before, as you are perfectly well aware.'

Caroline recoiled instinctively from the icy rage that throbbed beneath the outward formality of his words.

'Perhaps you would care to take a stroll with Miss Adams,' said the Dowager, who had once again turned conveniently deaf. 'She's a charming gal and might manage to smooth a few of your ruffled feathers.'

He did not wait for Caroline to give her consent to this suggestion, but turned and seized her arm, only to be foiled in his attempt to remove her from the box by the entry of a veritable army of the Dowager's elderly cronies. The visitors stared at Caroline with avid curiosity, scarcely masking their scrutiny even as they went through the elaborate rituals of greeting. Caroline, forgetting that Lord Carrisford was the man who had betrayed her stepbrother, curled her hand around his arm in silent supplication. Just for a moment she felt the warm pressure of his hand tightening around her fingers, then he was moving forward, smiling suavely at a middle-aged lady whose bounteous curves were somewhat inadequately stuffed into a gown of gentian-blue satin. 'Lady Baxter,' he murmured. 'How good of you to honour my mother with a visit. I *know* how much you dislike stirring from your seat during a performance. Mama! May I draw your attention to Lady Baxter? Miss Adams and I are leaving now to execute the errand you requested of us.'

In full view of the scandalised Lady Baxter and her attendant minions, he drew Caroline's hand tenderly through his arm. 'Shall we go, my love?' he enquired politely as he gave a dignified half-bow in the general direction of the assembled throng. She scarcely had time to nod her head before she was swept firmly from the box.

'Really, my lord,' Caroline expostulated, flustered by the gentleness of his touch, even though she tried to remind herself that his demonstartions of affection were all part of the act. 'Would you say that the methods you adopt are a trifle ruthless?'

He stopped in the middle of the corridor. 'I beg your pardon. I imagined that you wished to leave that rapacious group of gossip-mongers. Allow me to escort you back to my mother's box immediately.'

'You know very well that I wanted to leave,' she said snappishly, while all the time her heart beat out an erratic and joyful reminder that it was *his* hand clasping her finger-tips; *his* arm that gave her such powerful support; *his* swift steps that cleared a path through the chattering throng of playgoers.

'Why did you not let me know where you had gone?' His harsh question cut across her wistful thoughts, jerking her out of a pleasant daydream and back into chilly reality.

Her body stiffened as she remembered why she had run away and what this man had done to her brother. She glared at him fiercely.

'Why did you wish to find me, my lord? Was it to tell me that your treachery was all for the best? That I need not worry if I was instrumental in securing my own brother's arrest? After all, I'm sure you found Philippe's crime very wicked and, as far as you were concerned, there were no extenuating circumstances to explain his lapse. Is *that* what you wanted to tell me?'

'We cannot speak of such matters here,' he said, and his voice betrayed his exasperation. He pulled her roughly in the direction of a curtained alcove, his eyes making a restless search of the crowded lobby. Finally, he stopped a passing footman and pressgd a coin into the man's hand. 'See that we are not disturbed,' he said. The footman inspected the golden guinea solemnly, a slow grin spreading across his stolid features. For half that sum he would have barred the alcove entrance to King George himself. He sat down on a chair outside the plush curtains and whistled surreptitiously through the gap in his front teeth.

On the other side of the curtains, Lord Carrisford was deeply occupied in examining the gold buttons glistening on his waistcoat. 'I know that you do not care for *my* feelings,' he said at last, 'but you could have spared a thought for your brother. He was like a madman when we discovered that you had vanished from Carrisford House.'

'It did not seem to me, sir, that my brother was overly anxious to pursue our relationship just at that moment.'

Lord Carrisford spoke haughtily. 'Naturally, I explained to your stepbrother that his conclusions about us were false. Philippe soon realised that you had been an innocent victim of other people's scheming.'

'Naturally. Were your explanations given before or after you contrived to have Philippe arrested, my lord?'

'Are you never willing to give me the benefit of the doubt?' he snapped. 'Philippe has been taken to the Tower, it is true. But he is charged with no crime, nor will he be. His incarceration is for his own safety.'

'When we called on Madame la Comtesse this afternoon we heard from her own butler that she had been out all day striving to get Philippe released from prison.'

'Your stepmother is a talented actress, Caroline. You, of all people, should know that. She is aware of the true facts and is merely playing the rôle of a distracted mother. M. Patin keeps her under close observation, and the pretence is necessary. Although this is hardly an appropriate time or place, I will try to give you some explanation which will relieve the worst of your anxiety.'

She sat down, hope and dread warring within her. 'Tell me exactly what has happened to my brother, my lord. I am so tired of half-truths and promises.'

'Philippe is not under arrest. The warrant Lord Liverpool issued was merely a ruse I devised to get rid of M. Patin. Patin is already making preparations to return to France because he thinks his plot has succeeded. He believes Philippe has been arrested as a spy and, most important, he thinks I trust the despatches coming from Count André. As soon as Patin has returned to France Philippe will be smuggled out of the Tower and sent to some quiet spot in the country. He can lie low for a few weeks, and I will continue to sent Count André enthusiastic messages. Meanwhile, Wellington will base his strategic planning on his own military intelligence reports. Thus we can hope one more Bonapartist plot will be foiled.'

'You seem to have forgotten about Philippe's father. He still languishes in a French prison.'

'I believe he was executed twenty years ago, Caroline. I am awaiting couriers from France who will almost certainly confirm that the Count de la Rivière has been dead for years.'

Caroline stirred uneasily on the hard chair. 'But what if you are wrong, my lord?' she whispered. 'The life of Philippe's father will be forfeit because of you.'

He placed his hand gently beneath her chin and tilted her face up so that he could look deep into her eyes. 'My dear, you cannot believe that Napoleon's government would set him free, even if he is still alive? What have they to gain by such a move?'

'Then it is useless to hope?'

'You should hope, as your stepmother

does, that Philippe's father died at the time of the Terror. Freedom now could not compensate the Count for twenty years spent in a revolutionary prison.'

'I suppose not.' Caroline dashed away an obstinate tear. 'Poor Philippe. Poor Belle-mère. How wicked of M. Patin to revive so many old hurts.'

'That is hardly the greatest of his crimes, my dear.' With a groan, he bent down to look at her. 'Don't cry, Caroline. I can't bear it when you cry!' With a finger he traced the path of the tear down her cheek. 'Has nobody ever told you that it is against the law to be able to cry without ruining your complexion?' His hand dropped back to his side, but she did not turn away for she thought she detected a warm glow half-hidden in the depths of his eyes.

As he stared down at her, she saw the glow fade, to be replaced by a deep, searching look. Suddenly he pulled her up from the chair, placing his arms gently around her and pulling her unresisting body close to his own. He brushed his mouth across her lips, and this time she did not pretend to herself that his kiss was unwelcome. 'Caroline . . .'

'Ahem. Sir. Miss.' The muffled voice of

the footman sounded from behind the curtains. 'The play has already started again and I oughta be pushing along. I dunno if you was wanting to see any more of it. Miserable old story I calls it. Every one of 'em dead at the end.'

'I quite agree with you,' said Lord Carrisford shortly. 'We have no intention of returning to see the rest of it. But you may go, if you have to.'

He spoke briskly to Caroline. 'We cannot stay here any longer. Let me escort you back to my mother's house.'

'This evening's outing with your mother was intended to restore my reputation, my lord. I cannot think that it has so far served the purpose.'

'To the devil with your reputation, Caroline! Come with me, there is so much I want to say to you.'

She pulled away from him, angry that she had allowed herself to succumb once again to the fascination of his presence. 'How easy it is for you to cast away my reputation! It may be of no importance to you, but I shall find myself destitute if I do not make some effort to re-establish myself in the eyes of the world.'

He looked at her oddly and gave a short

little laugh. 'Since I am responsible for your public ruin, may I be allowed to make restitution? Will you do me the honour, Miss Adams, of becoming my wife?'

She turned away quickly, to mask the hope that sprang into her eyes. 'I find such jesting the height of bad form, my lord,' she said breathlessly.

He gave another odd laugh. 'I am not jesting, my dear. My proposal was made very much in earnest.'

The colour fluctuated in her cheeks and she could feel the uneven rise and fall of her breast. 'You feel *obliged* to offer for me, my lord, is that it?' she asked. She kept her face hidden so that he would not be able to see how desperately she longed to hear him deny the accusation. If only he would tell her that he loved her!

That was an absurd dream, of course. His voice was quite cold when he answered her. 'I am sorry that you have such a low impression of my motives. I hoped your feelings for me had undergone some change since our first meeting, but I see I was mistaken. You have now made your feelings perfectly clear, Miss Adams. I can only regret that I have, on two separate occasions, forced repugnant proposals upon you. It will not happen again, I assure you. May I be allowed to escort you back to my mother's box?'

She reached out her hand and almost touched him before common sense reasserted itself. Her own love was so strong that she longed to throw herself in his arms and admit she would marry him on any terms at all, even though he shared none of her feelings. But she could not allow herself to take advantage of his generosity; she loved him too much for that. A deep, mutual affection was the only justification for entering into such an unequal match, and since love was lacking on his side a marriage between them must be impossible.

The decision was hard to reach, and even harder for Caroline to adhere to. She could not trust herself to speak for a while, but simply nodded her head and brushed quickly past him before the tears could start to fall. Her arm accidentally pressed against his rigid shoulders, and she flinched away before he could feel the tremor of passion that flickered through her. 'Let us go, my lord,' she said huskily.

He led her swiftly along the brightly-lighted corridors, deserted now that the play had recommenced. Her blind gaze fixed itself upon branches of blazing candles, ornately-gilded mirrors, anywhere but on the man at her side. At last they reached the sanctuary of the Dowager's box.

'I will take leave of you here, Miss Adams.' His voice was remote, she supposed from relief at his narrow escape. He scrutinised the deathly pallor of her face and, just for a moment, his expression softened. 'You look exhausted, my dear. The activities of the past few days have been too much for you.'

She could not bear to hear the unaccustomed kindness in his voice. She was afraid it would shatter the precarious control she retained over her emotions.

'It is nothing,' she said. 'A night's rest will soon refresh me.'

He did not reply, but lifted her hand to his lips and then, as if compelled almost against his better judgment, pressed a swift, hard kiss against her gloved palm.

'Goodbye, Miss Adams. I shall see to it that your stepbrother is well cared for.'

'If his safety is in your hands, my lord, I know that he is well protected,' she said softly.

He turned away, as if impatient at her words, and tapped on the door of the box.

She smiled at him in farewell, a bright, impersonal smile that gave no hint of the painful ache constricting her throat and stopping her speaking. The maid opened the door, while Carrisford still stared at her, and Caroline, with a brief wave of her hand, slipped silently into the welcome darkness of the Dowager's box.

Chapter Sixteen

'I HAVE come to say goodbye, Belle-mère, and to tell you that I plan to join my father's cousins in Harrogate. I could not leave without giving you my love, and sending Philippe my best wishes for his future happiness.'

The Comtesse wrung her hands together in a frantic gesture Caroline could not understand. She saw that her stepmother's face looked pale beneath its usual layer of maquillage.

'You can't leave London while Philippe is in prison!' exclaimed the Comtesse.

Caroline stared at her stepmother. 'But Philippe is quite safe,' she said. 'Lord Carrisford told me last night that his imprisonment was all a ruse. It was just a plot to deceive M. Patin.'

As soon as she had spoken she realised the significance of the Comtesse's frantic gestures. Too late, she understood that they could be overheard. She tried desperately to think how she could retrieve her disastrous error, but M. Patin was already walking into the room. Caroline shivered involuntarily as she saw him. How could she ever have been foolish enough to consider him an insignificant man?

'Miss Adams.' He bowed to her, smiling with every appearance of unruffled good humour. 'You have just confirmed what I have been suspecting for some time. Lord Carrisford is noted for his shrewdness, and I have been wondering why he swallowed all my lies so readily. Now I have my answer. He has not been deceived at all, but has been tricking me with as neat a scheme as I have encountered in a long while.' His voice expressed frank admiration for Lord Carrisford's powers of deception. 'The only remaining point of interest is whether or not something may yet be salvaged from the wreck. One does so hope, for the sake of Madame la Comtesse and her husband, that we may be able to devise some method of tricking Lord Carrisford.'

'We have done our best to fulfil our part of the bargain,' said the Comtesse. 'Is this how Napoleon keeps his promises to those who are in his power?'

For a moment, M. Patin's mask of courtesy slipped, and his mouth twisted in a savage snarl of rage. 'The Emperor does not concern himself with the scum left over from the corrupt governments of the Royalist tyranny,' he spat out.

'Why, then, does he keep my husband behind bars? Is twenty years of imprisonment insufficient to expiate for the sin of urging moderation upon King Louis?'

M. Patin's brief anger was once more under control. 'Enough,' he said. 'This conversation is without point. I have decided what must be done.' A slow smile of satisfaction stretched across his face. 'I find there is a certain delicious irony in the situation. Lord Carrisford no longer trusts me or Count André. The information in André's despatches will be totally ignored. So I shall see to it that André's despatches contain only the truth. What exquisite subtlety of deception! Lord Carrisford's advice will be so bad that I don't doubt that at the end of this little episode he will find his reputation and career shattered beyond repair.'

'And what will happen to my husband?' whispered the Comtesse.

'Your husband?' repeated Patin impatiently. 'I daresay, Madame, that if you are wise enough to keep your mouth firmly shut your husband will be returned to you. Of course, one word to Lord Carrisford, one whisper even, and your husband . . . Well, I fear that life would not be very pleasant for the Count. In his weakened state of health . . .' M. Patin allowed his voice to die away in a regretful murmur.

The Comtesse turned away and stood staring over the bleak courtyard. Caroline, meanwhile, shrank back against the sofa cushions, hoping M. Patin might forget her presence in the room. She kept her gaze averted from him, but she felt a sickening churning in her stomach and knew that his pale brown eyes rested contemplatively on the golden profusion of her hair.

'There is only one problem remaining in my excellent planning,' he said. 'You, Miss Adams, will without doubt take the first opportunity to run to your lover with this whole story. I could kill you, of course.'

For a few minutes he studied her speculatively, and Caroline read the cold appraisal of a professional killer in the ruthless efficiency of his gaze. 'It seems a pity to waste such an eminently saleable piece of merchandise, and I couldn't kill you here, of course. If I am forced to take you with me in order to dispose of you, I may as well reap some personal benefit from the inconvenience.' He straightened, his mind evidently made up. 'Miss Adams, you are about to discover what civilised living is all about. I shall take you back with me to France, thus killing two birds with one small stone. *You* will be unable to report the details of my plan to Lord Carrisford, and I . . . Yes, I think I shall make a present of you to my friend André. Straight to André's bed from Lord Carrisford's. Oh yes, that is a splendid joke, is it not? I assure you, André will appreciate it to the full.'

'You do not imagine that you can abduct me from the Comtesse's own home in broad daylight and in full view of the servants?' Caroline did not try to conceal her scorn.

M. Patin laughed gently. 'Oh yes, I rather think I can. You will come willingly, you know, or else I can promise the Comtesse she will never see her husband or her son again.'

Caroline looked at the rigid back of the Comtesse, who was still turned obstinately away from her stepdaughter and M. Patin. She longed to run to the Comtesse and whisper some words of reassurance, to apologise for her thoughtlessness in bringing them both to such a pass, and to cry out her conviction that M. le Comte was already dead. But a dreadful fear prevented her from taking the risk. The Comtesse already blamed herself for leaving France without her husband. What if Lord Carrisford were mistaken and the Count languished in a French prison? Caroline could not bear to live with his death upon her conscience. She did not doubt for one minute that M. Patin would take pleasure in carrying out his threats if she or the Comtesse attempted to trick him any further.

Her thoughts skittered feverishly around the options available to her. Once she surrendered herself to M. Patin's power her best chance of escape would be during their wait for a boat. M. Patin could not be expecting to make tonight's tide, and if they were left for several hours in one of the Channel ports Caroline tried to convince herself that some chance of escape was bound to occur. Having decided upon her immediate course of action, she looked at M. Patin with a creditable pretence of indifference.

'La, sir, it's all one to me whether I go or stay now that I know Philippe is safe. Whether France is ruled by Napoleon or King Louis, I still have to find some way of buttering my bread.' She shrugged her shoulders. 'One man is much the same as another in the dark. Count André . . . Lord Carrisford . . . they are just names.'

She could feel his piercing eyes examining her closely, so she tossed back her hair and turned her face up defiantly to his inspection. She spared a moment to bless the good fortune which had introduced her to M. Patin at Covent Garden theatre when she was decked out from head to foot in gaudy jewels. He had no reason to suspect that she was anything other than Lord Carrisford's mistress and available to the highest bidder.

Her reckless words seemed to satisfy him, for he turned immediately to the Comtesse, dismissing Caroline from his thoughts without bothering to speak to her again.

'Miss Adams will come with me. I rely upon your good sense, Madame la Comtesse, to keep this afternoon's events a secret between the three of us. When next you have word from me, Madame, it will be to send you notification of M. le Comte's arrival in England. Let us hope that Carrisford behaves in a way that justifies the Count's early release.'

'I pray he will,' said the Comtesse dispiritedly. 'You may rest assured he will learn nothing from me.' Her shoulders drooped in defeat. 'When will you and Caroline be leaving? Is it permitted for my maid to pack her a change of clothing?'

'She can change her clothes when we are safely in France,' said M. Patin curtly. 'I plan to leave town at once, before Carrisford decides to pay you a call. He might even suffer a change of heart and decide against allowing me to leave the country. It is better if we set out for the coast at once.'

Caroline pouted petulantly. 'But I cannot just get up and walk from this room straight into a travelling chaise.'

'Can you not? I think you will be amazed at the things you will learn to do over the next few months.' M. Patin turned towards the Comtesse. 'My bags are already packed, Madame. Tell one of the footmen to carry them to your carriage.'

At last the Comtesse turned away from the window. 'You overstep the mark, M. Patin, when you speak to me in such a fashion. My memory is long, and I clearly recall the days when you would have hesitated to address a single remark to me before I acknowledged your presence.'

M. Patin allowed the hatred to flare into his cold expression. 'My memory is equally as long, citizen. Did you not realise the pleasure I have derived from this particular assignment? How noble you were in those days before the Revolution, and how humble we were pleased to be in your presence!' His eyes blazed with fanatic cruelty. 'My heart pounds with joy every time I issue an order to you, Madame, and it almost bursts when I see that order obeyed. Summon the horses from the stables, Madame. Time presses.'

The Comtesse's brief moment of defiance seemed to be over as quickly as it had flared up, and she walked over to the bell-rope to call a servant.

'M. Patin and Miss Adams wish to go out,' she said tonelessly to the footman who answered her summons. 'Tell Jem to bring round my carriage. M. Patin is in a hurry.'

M. Patin sat down and smiled at them

cordially. 'Excellent,' he said. 'Let us all be comfortable while we are waiting. No, no, Madame, pray do not leave us.' His hand closed gently around the Comtesse's wrist. 'I shall enjoy having a conversation with you.'

'You can force me to stay here, Patin, but you cannot force me to speak.'

'You think not?' He shrugged. 'We will not pursue the point. Perhaps, Miss Adams, you would care for some refreshment. It is a long way to Dover.'

She shook her head, and they all three sat in silence until the footman at last returned. 'Madam,' he announced. 'Your carriage is waiting for the visitors.'

It was dark when M. Patin assisted Caroline into a carriage at the first stop on the post-road to Dover. At his insistence she was wrapped in a drab grey travelling-cloak that covered the bright gold of her hair and concealed the elegant lines of her figure. There was little hope that their departure would be remembered by any of the overworked stable-hands in the busy posting-yard.

M. Patin had experienced no difficulty in keeping Caroline under control. His French valet, whose slim figure belied the wiry strength of his body, acted as a guard. The valet never moved from Caroline's side. His hand gripped her arm, not in support, but rather as a silent threat. He had pulled the folds of her cape around the sharp steel blade of a Spanish stiletto, and its point was aimed straight at her heart.

Now, two hours into their journey, she wondered how she could have been so foolish as to imagine that she would ever escape from M. Patin. He was an experienced veteran of a score of similar missions, while she had never even visited the Channel coast of England.

She had no plan of escape in mind, so there was little point in trying to find out exactly where they were. Nevertheless, she concentrated upon the route they were following so as to take her mind off other, less pleasant, trains of thought. From what she could see through the darkness, she thought they might be travelling through the deserted stretch of countryside between Chatham and Sittingbourne. If so, they were making excellent time.

Neither Patin nor Jacques, the valet, said anything to her and, had it not been for the knife pressed against her ribs, she would have thought she was forgotten. The silence in the carriage began to press in upon her and suddenly she looked directly at M. Patin.

'M. le Comte de la Rivière is dead, is he not?' She blurted out the first question that sprang into her head, and then was appalled at this second example of thoughtlessness within such a short space of time.

M. Patin observed her dispassionately. 'Why should you think such a thing?'

Once again she tried to cover up her error. 'Why should Robespierre have saved him? He executed all the other aristocrats who had served on King Louis' Council.'

The pale eyes stared at her meditatively. 'Does it make any difference to you whether the Count is alive or dead?'

She feigned indifference, lifting her shoulders in a slight shrug. 'I have never seen the Count, and I shall never see the Comtesse again. Whether he is alive or dead will have no effect upon my life. I was simply curious. And bored. Long carriage rides with gloomy companions do not strike me as a very diverting way to spend my time.'

The blandness of M. Patin's expression was twisted by a brief flash of cruelty. 'M. le Comte is dead,' he said shortly. 'There is a certain subtle pleasure, do you not agree, in forcing Madame la Comtesse's hand with such an empty set of cards?'

She was spared the necessity of thinking up a suitable response by a sudden violent lurching of the carriage, swiftly followed by the explosion of a single gunshot. They could hear the terrified neighing of the horses as the drivers struggled to hold the rearing horses to the road.

'*Bandits!*' exclaimed Jacques in a hiss of surprise, and Caroline clenched her teeth tightly together to prevent herself crying out with fright. She wanted to escape from Patin, but not by falling victim to a gang of highwaymen.

M. Patin was too experienced a campaigner to show alarm at the sound of a single shot. He removed a pistol from the holster in the carriage wall and clicked back the safety lock of his weapon. He held the pistol in his right hand, balancing the barrel across his left arm, the muzzle pointing directly at the door handle. Jacques, equally calm, moved the knife-blade away from Caroline's side. He crouched down alongside the other carriage door, knife raised, ready to spring out at any intruder.

They had scarcely taken their positions before three more shots rang out, and they could hear the clatter of weapons being thrown on the ground as the coachman and the groom climbed down from their driving-perch. Caroline cringed back more deeply inside the heavy folds of her cape. Her fate, if captured by a gang of highwaymen, didn't bear thinking about.

The two doors of the carriage were suddenly wrenched open, and Caroline saw Jacques fall victim to a sharp blow delivered to the side of his head. Even as Jacques fell, she heard the shots ring out from the other side of the carriage, and she cried out as she saw M. Patin recoil, clutching his shoulder. The blood spurted out with frightening force, and he pressed his hand to the wound in a vain attempt to staunch the bleeding. She tore the sash from her dress for a make-shift bandage, unable to ignore his pain, even though she despised him.

The harsh voice of one of the highway-men boomed loudly in the still of the night. 'Not so fast there, pretty lady. Hold on just a moment, if you please.'

A pair of rough and dirty hands reached into the interior of the coach and grabbed her by the shoulders. They pulled her with brutal force out on to the grass verge and pushed back the hood which covered her face and hair. 'Well, I never! A veritable treasure!' The owner of the hands slapped his thigh with considerable self-satisfaction. 'Hey, Sir!' His loud voice was raised still louder. 'Step over this way, if you please, and see what I have found.'

The tall figure of their leader, mounted on a bay gelding, rode over to Caroline's side. He was clothed entirely in black and his face was covered by a leather mask. Only his eyes gleamed through two narrow slits in the black leather. He studied her with insolent appraisal, while all the time a pistol remained negligently trained upon her.

'She looks worth a closer examination.' He gestured to Caroline with his pistol. 'Come over here, wench, and let's see if you're worth taking up on *my* horse.'

She stared at the pistol, resting casually against the bay's saddle. The pearl handle gleamed with a familiar lustre, the shining silver of the barrel shimmered in the moonlight. She recognised one of her father's duelling pistols and swayed on the verge of fainting. She looked up into the brigand's face in time to catch a glint of laughter in the grey eyes staring out from behind the mask, and in the same instant she recognised Lord Carrisford. Before she could utter any betraying word she was swept up to the broad back of the gelding, her body held close within the protection of his arms.

For a few minutes she revelled in the luxury of feeling entirely safe and cherished. As if at a great distance she saw the band of highwaymen lock the travelling chaise with M. Patin and Jacques inside. The baggage, already strewn over the grass verge, was quickly rifled to convey the impression of a search for money and valuables. Almost before she had time to assimilate what the men were doing, a cry went up.

'Coach coming! Time to leave!'

She felt the rush of air as the men urged their horses to a gallop, Lord Carrisford in the lead. He soon pulled his mount in a sharp arc, plunging off the muddy highway and into a densely-wooded stretch of undergrowth. Their headlong pace slackened as the horses struggled to pass along the narrow path leading through the dark trees.

Lord Carrisford drew his band to a halt by a pond of stagnant water, hidden deep in the woods. He sprang down from the saddle, tossing the reins to one of his men, and then held his arms up to Caroline. She slid self-consciously to the ground. With a total disregard for the interested attention of his fellow-brigands, Carrisford ripped off his mask and crushed Caroline to him. He covered her face with kisses, and although she knew she would regret such heedless behaviour later, for the present she simply abandoned herself to the bliss of being kissed, hungrily and passionately, by the man she loved.

At last Lord Carrisford lifted his mouth from hers, although his arm remained tightly clasped about her waist, and with his spare hand he ruffled the tangled curls of her hair. He grinned at his men, not one whit put out by their observation of his recent activities.

'I would like you all to meet Miss Adams, my betrothed, whom you so gallantly helped to rescue,' he said. The men removed their masks and bobbed deferential bows, twisting their hats somewhat awkwardly in their hands.

'This is Thomas, my dear,' said Lord Carrisford, gesturing towards the stocky individual who had pulled Caroline from Patin's carriage. 'He is my gamekeeper, but he makes a convincing highwayman, don't you think?'

'Very convincing,' she returned dryly. 'I

hope I may never meet a more villainous villain.'

The gamekeeper spoke to her sheepishly. 'No offence, your ladyship. I just did what his lordship said. No disrespect intended. None in the world.'

'I am grateful for your help. May I know the names of the rest of the band?'

'Peter is my chief groom. Over there is Young Tom, and this is Arthur. They were both born on the estate. They looked quite dashing in their masks, did they not?'

'They looked terrifying,' said Caroline. 'But you saved my life, and I thank you all.'

Thomas growled to cover his embarrassment. 'Aye! And I wish we had killed this scoundrels that made away with you, ma'am. What's the point of letting rogues like that live to harm some other poor lady?'

'It is better this way,' said Lord Carrisford decisively. 'Patin, if he survives the gunshot wound, will think that he fell victim to common highway robbers. I prefer him to remain ignorant of my part in the affair. I am going to take Miss Adams back to Carrisford Park now. Thomas, I shall leave you men to see to the horses and to dispose of our disguises as you think best.'

He smiled slightly. 'Perhaps a small bonfire?'

Without giving Caroline a chance to speak, he bent down and swept her up into his arms. 'My curricle is just a short distance away, my love. We shall soon be back at my house, where my mother and your stepmother are waiting anxiously.' He bent down and whispered mockingly, so that only she could hear, 'You see how careful I am to observe the proprieties for my betrothed.'

'I am not your betrothed,' she hissed. 'And please put me down. I can walk.'

'Of course you can, but why not pretend a little?' he said as he strode towards the edge of the wood. 'It is such an excellent excuse for holding you in my arms.'

She was unable to think of any scathing retort, chiefly because she was fully occupied in thinking how delightful it was to be pressed so close to Lord Carrisford's heart. At first she held her hands pressed primly to her bosom, but when she realised that neither this, nor any other half-hearted gesture, was going to make Lord Carrisford set her down, she gave up the foolish attempt to assert her independence and reached her arms up to clasp lovingly around his neck.

Since Lord Carrisford was ungentleman-like enough to construe this gesture as an invitation to indulge in further kisses of a highly improper variety, their progress towards the waiting curricle was seriously delayed. Neither Lord Carrisford nor Caroline seemed to consider the delay particularly regrettable.

The edge of the wood was finally reached, however, and the carriage immediately sighted. A young boy held the horses still while Lord Carrisford placed Caroline tenderly on the seat, piling cushions and rugs all around her.

'You may go and find the rest of the men,' said Lord Carrisford to the stable-hand. 'They could probably use an extra pair of hands to take care of Imperator.'

'Yes, my lord.' The boy ran off into the woods, well pleased to exchange the prospect of perching behind a curricle for the more exciting prospect of actually mounting his lordship's famous bay. Lord Carrisford waited until the boy was out of hearing, then said. 'Would you like to talk a little, or are you too tired.'

'I am not tired,' said Caroline, opening her eyes and shooting up on her seat. 'We should certainly talk, my lord. I have to thank you most sincerely for rescuing me so cleverly from the consequences of my own folly and for concocting that . . . that . . . story about a betrothal for the benefit of the servants. I am deeply appreciative of all you have done for me, my lord.'

'Richard,' he said absently. 'Now that we are betrothed I really do think you should call me Richard.'

'But we are not betrothed!' cried Caroline in exasperation. 'Pray, my lord, be sensible.'

'Very well, we shall be sensible,' he said, and Caroline suppressed a quiver of disappointment that her point had been so quickly won. 'Tell me if you discovered anything from M. Patin,' said Carrisford.

'I have found out that the Comte de la Rivière is dead,' she said. 'M. Patin admitted as much to me. He was actually proud of tricking the Comtesse.' She shuddered. 'He is an evil man.

'Yes, I rather think he is.' Carrisford saw that she was distressed, and said with deliberate lightness, 'Do you not wish to hear how I achieved your daring rescue?'

'Yes, please. I can scarcely believe even now how quickly you discovered our trail.'

'You have the Comtesse to thank for that.

She realised that neither she nor her servants could prevent Patin abducting you, at least without risk of injury, but she scarcely waited for Patin to take you out of the house before she jumped into a hackney and came in search of me. She discovered me at my mother's house. You will remember that Patin said he was heading for Dover, a logical destination since it is the closest point to the French coast. Since my principle estate lies close to the main Dover road it did not require much ingenuity to come up with our plan.'

She touched his hand in a gesture of gratitude. 'I don't believe that your plan was quite as easy to execute as you try to make out. I don't like to think about the risks you all ran in disabling Patin and his assistant.'

'I was trained by Wellington,' he said lightly. 'You can at least expect me to mount an efficient military campaign, even if my affairs of the heart have been less successful.'

She did not answer, and Carrisford spoke to her softly. 'You have not asked why the Comtesse found me at my mother's house. Would you not like to hear what my mother was saying to me?'

'Your conversations with your mother are

naturally not intended for my ears, my lord.'

'You think not? Well, I imagine everybody else in her house heard what she had to say, for she repeated her message at least three times and all at the top of her lungs. She wanted to know why I hadn't married you. She said you'd talked a great deal of nonsense to her about leaving London and going to Harrogate. Her opinion of the Harrogate cousins, I am happy to say, is as unfavourable as my own. It is most unflattering of you to keep mentioning that dreary spa as an alternative to a perfectly respectable position as my wife.'

'But what would your friends say if you married me? You cannot pretend it is a conventional or a suitable match.'

'I am neither a conventional nor a suitable man, my love. It is enough for me to know that I love you. As for the opinion of my friends—I imagine most of the men will be wildly envious. The women, of course, will all find you monstrously unsuitable. But they would find you unsuitable if you were the daughter of the Archbishop of Canterbury. Nobody with your looks could ever hope to be accepted by society's matrons. Remember they have daughters and nieces of their own to marry off!' His eyes crinkled with the suspicion of a smile. 'I shall do my best to rectify that unfortunate situation. I shall keep you *enceinte* for the first few years we are married, and with luck you will sink into middle age looking no more than pretty.'

She pressed her hands to her burning cheeks. 'I don't know what to say.'

'Well, I wish you would decide upon something pretty quickly, for we are approaching the house, and I can see that there is a large welcoming party already standing out on the steps to greet us.'

'You know I ought to say no.'

'Only if you don't love me.' With admirable driving skill he controlled the horses with one hand, while pulling Caroline gently round to face him. 'Well, Caroline. Is that why you won't marry me? Because you don't love me?'

'You know it is not,' she whispered. 'I think I have loved you almost since the first night we met.'

'And I have loved you ever since I saw you tucked up in my bed,' he said wickedly. 'No, no! Pray consider the horses!' Lord Carrisford drew the curricle to a halt, and said firmly, 'I consider the matter settled.

We shall be married tomorrow. There is no reason to wait. I need to be in Vienna three weeks from today, and I have a special licence waiting on my desk in the library.'

'But Richard . . .'

'Hush.'

With great presence of mind, Lord Carrisford put a stop to any further protestations by kissing Caroline in a manner that left no breath for arguments. It was several minutes before she leaned back against his waistcoat and said with singular lack of conviction, 'We cannot get married tomorrow, Richard. I have nothing to wear.'

'That, my love, must be accounted almost the best news I have heard all day.'

She tried hard to sound disapproving, although her heart was bursting with happiness. 'And that, my lord, was a most improper betrothal speech.'

'But nowhere near as improper as my feelings,' he rejoined promptly.

Caroline, recognising at last that Lord Carrisford's moral sensibilities were blunted beyond repair, gave up the lonely struggle for reform and abandoned herself to the enjoyment of his depravity.